KT-500-611

SPECIAL MESSAGE TO READERS

This book is published under the auspices of

THE ULVERSCROFT FOUNDATION

(registered charity No. 264873 UK)

Established in 1972 to provide funds for research, diagnosis and treatment of eye diseases. Examples of contributions made are: —

A Children's Assessment Unit at Moorfield's Hospital, London.

•

Twin operating theatres at the Western Ophthalmic Hospital, London.

•

A Chair of Ophthalmology at the Royal Australian College of Ophthalmologists.

•

The Ulverscroft Children's Eye Unit at the Great Ormond Street Hospital For Sick Children, London.

You can help further the work of the Foundation by making a donation or leaving a legacy. Every contribution, no matter how small, is received with gratitude. Please write for details to:

THE ULVERSCROFT FOUNDATION,
The Green, Bradgate Road, Anstey,
Leicester LE7 7FU, England.
Telephone: (0116) 236 4325

In Australia write to:
THE ULVERSCROFT FOUNDATION,
c/o The Royal Australian and New Zealand
College of Ophthalmologists,
94-98 Chalmers Street, Surry Hills,
N.S.W. 2010, Australia

Guy Fraser lives on the Isle of Bute.

BLADE OF THE ASSASSIN

1863. The Detective Department at Glasgow Central is undermanned and short of funds, yet Superintendent Jarrett, Inspector Grant and Sergeant Quinn are expected to run to ground a multiple murderer, a vengeful madman and a professional pornographer. Henry Jarrett depends solely on deduction, whilst Inspector Charlie Grant brings to bear his experience of the city's back streets. Tommy Quinn for his part is at home with the recently introduced technologies of crime scene photography and the electric telegraph. Together, they uncover a huge conspiracy — the proportions of which could shake the political administrations on both sides of the Atlantic.

GUY FRASER

BLADE OF THE ASSASSIN

Complete and Unabridged

ULVERSCROFT
Leicester

First published in Great Britain in 2007 by
Robert Hale Limited
London

First Large Print Edition
published 2008
by arrangement with
Robert Hale Limited
London

The moral right of the author has been asserted

Copyright © 2007 by Guy Fraser
All rights reserved

British Library CIP Data

Fraser, Guy
Blade of the assassin.—Large print ed.—
Ulverscroft large print series: crime
1. Police—Scotland—Glasgow—Fiction 2. Murder —Investigation—Scotland—Glasgow—Fiction 3. Glasgow (Scotland)—Social conditions—19th century—Fiction 4. Detective and mystery stories 5. Large type books
I. Title
823.9′2 [F]

ISBN 978–1–84782–325–0

Published by
F. A. Thorpe (Publishing)
Anstey, Leicestershire

Set by Words & Graphics Ltd.
Anstey, Leicestershire
Printed and bound in Great Britain by
T. J. International Ltd., Padstow, Cornwall

This book is printed on acid-free paper

1

The man who thought he was being pursued half-ran, half-stumbled along the irregular pavement, occasionally catching a raised flagstone with the toe of his boot and almost falling. As he loped along he somehow managed to locate the armholes of his coat and tugged the garment around him without even attempting to fasten any of the numerous buttons. Every now and again he would risk a quick glance over his shoulder to see if that wild devil was chasing him. Even though he was nowhere to be seen the fleeing man knew he wouldn't give up that easily. The madman knew these grim Glasgow streets and every alley between them, while the hunted one was a stranger, not only to this city, but even to these shores.

The blow to his cheek was beginning to sting now. At first he had scarcely noticed it, because so much was happening all at once. The woman was yelling, sometimes at him, sometimes at the crazed devil, amid the clatter of pewter plates and the smashing of cheap cups. Most of the latter were already cracked and chipped. Now they were useless shards, upwardly curving and malicious on the dusty floor.

When the one who considered himself ill-done by and the victim of the piece reached the railway arches, the echoing boots seemed to menace him from all sides. And it was dark. Out there in the empty cobble-stoned streets the dawn light made hurrying possible, but within the arches it was another matter. There were so many coal-black shadows in which anything might be lurking, waiting to pounce, and unfortunately he had to pass through one in particular to reach the dockland. The howling banshee knew where he was going and exactly how to beat him to it.

When it came it was utterly without warning. A hand snaked out of the darkness and cupped the nape of the neck, pulling him forward to meet his fate. In that same instant the finely crafted blade buried itself deep in his heart, dispatching him instantly.

The killer had been waiting in the pitch darkness just long enough to gain his night-sight. When the body was lowered to the ground he quickly went through every pocket. There wasn't a great deal, but he took whatever he could find, however worthless. Then he checked his dead man's fingers for rings and his neck for a chain or medallion.

Since there was no one else around, and the beat constable was not due back this way for another hour or so, he departed the scene in an unhurried manner. That way if he did happened to be noticed very little about him would be remembered.

* * *

Being instinctively territorial, Mrs Maitland's four gentleman boarders each occupied the same small corner table in the dining parlour every morning and every evening. No one would have considered for a moment encroaching on another's space, so such conversations as occurred were carried out in a clipped and to-the-point manner across the no-man's land that was the good lady's deep cherry carpet. As ever, Lizzie the sole maid and general dogsbody, swept silently from table to table, and in and out of the large room, oblivious to the talk and unnoticed because of her plain, colourless uniform.

'Gettysburg,' Mr Sweetman stated, shaking his head. The battle had ended a mere twelve days ago, on 3 July in this year of 1863, yet already a full report of it was given in the daily press. Not that long before it would have taken weeks, and sometimes months, for the report of some distant victory or calamity to reach these shores. Now, with steamboat companies intent only on breaking records, news really was news, not rapidly cooling history. The world was shrinking and dangers no longer seemed far off and unthreatening.

For a few moments no one responded to the traveller's attempt at tearing apart the shroud of silence, mainly because there was little to say about such carnage that produced no obvious outcome, but also because the other three diners had little time for Sweetman or his inexhaustible fund of jokes. Then the assistant bank manager, Mr Croall, said simply, 'Shocking. A dreadful waste. And for what?'

At the table closest to the door, Mr Trimmer, the gaunt and humourless bookseller, spared young Croall a brief glance.

'As I read it,' he said, 'it was not entirely inconclusive. It rather looks as though the tide is turning against the Confederacy, although I should imagine that it is not as your bank would have wished.'

Croall laid his knife and fork on his plate and stared down at his unfinished breakfast herrings. If at all possible, he disliked the pasty-faced Trimmer more than Sweetman, even though the latter was now bending forward and grinning in anticipation of an argument arising out of his solitary utterance.

'And why might that be?' Croall asked, without so much as a glance in Trimmer's direction.

'Oh, come now, my dear fellow. Name me the bank or the merchant in this city who does not support the efforts of the slave states. May the good Lord help you if Lincoln prevails.'

'Are you telling me that you wouldn't mind paying the earth and the moon for your cotton garments? Because that's what a Northern victory would mean.'

Whatever Mr Trimmer was about to say perished in his throat as the fourth man in the room gently tapped the side of his cup with his knife to indicate his desire for a little peace and quiet during breakfast. Superintendent Henry Jarrett of the Detective Department at Glasgow Central had more on his mind than a foreign war, however relevant the outcome might be to the price of goods in the market-place.

Of medium height and indeterminate age, the clean-shaven Jarrett was quite unremarkable, yet he exuded an air of authority acquired and finely honed during his years with the Hong Kong police. There, a small mixed-race force of British, Indian and native Chinese were faced with the almost impossible task of combating the gambling syndicates, vice rings and pirate gangs to whom murder was a way of life.

He was, to date, a bachelor, set in his ways yet not entirely unyielding. It was true that no one was permitted to polish his boots, because no one could meet his exacting demands. Neither was anyone allowed to clean the windows of his Wardian case, within which nestled a variety of small ferns, protected from the coal smoke and sulphuric acid of this industrial city. It was a small haven of peace into which he would gaze for a spell each evening, and it served not only to relax him after the ugliness of the day, but also to focus and collate his thoughts. More than one problem had been solved in contemplation of that tiny, deep-green forest.

But it was here, in the dining parlour, that Jarrett's specific requirements were most likely to be observed by interested parties. Conventional teas and coffees were not acceptable. Rather, his chosen beverage was the Iron Goddess of Mercy — Ti Kuan Yin — in his estimation the finest of the Black Dragon teas. He would regularly collect a pound of the leaf from McKillop the China tea importer and convey it to Mrs Maitland, who had long since learnt that it must be infused in hot water, never boiling. His only other demand was that his toast should be cut thickly, uniformly golden brown, buttered to the edges and presented to him along with a pot of Keiller's marmalade. Apart from these small matters he was really quite easy-going. He would not, for example, ever dream of even attempting to enforce his personal wish that there should be no smoking in the dining areas. The fact that nobody did may or may not have been coincidental.

Jarrett had long since discovered that the simple act of bringing out his silver hunter, springing it open and consulting it with a pronounced frown was worth a thousand words. It said that he was running a little late and that he would have to get a move on if he proposed to catch Menzies' eye-catching Tartan Bus before it set off. Not that it really would leave without him. Driver Hutchins and Conductor MacNair were as unflappable as the two traffic-hardened horses that pulled the open-topped conveyance. They knew the superintendent well and would always give him that little bit of extra time if he needed it. And on the rare occasions when he would be held up indefinitely, Lizzie would be sent scurrying to pass on his message.

As it happens, this was going to be one of those mornings. Jarrett had just closed his watch case and was in the act of returning it to his waistcoat pocket when Mrs Maitland swept into the room and made a beeline for him.

'Mr Jarrett,' she said softly, since it was no one else's business, 'there's a young constable to speak with you. As he is in uniform I didn't know whether to put him in the kitchen or the drawing-room.'

Jarrett smiled at this strange confusion.

'So where did you put him, Mrs Maitland?' he asked.

'The drawing-room, since he is on an errand of some importance.'

'And do you happen to know the nature of this important errand?'

'Oh no, Mr Jarrett,' the good lady said, in a way that suggested she would never care to pry into matters that were none of her concern. 'I merely assume it to be important. The young man seems a little agitated.'

Constable MacLean may have been somewhat ill at ease because he was out of his natural environment in a room like this. He had clearly been placed here but not invited to sit. Pleasant and obliging though Mrs Maitland was, she never forgot for a single moment that she was the relict of a middle-class corn merchant and not only knew her own place in the world, but everyone else's too.

Although the superintendent had never laid eyes on this particular young officer before he could tell immediately that the lad was destined for promotion. He drew himself up to his full height, which was a good half a head taller than Jarrett himself, and held his helmet in the regulation manner under the crook of his right arm with the coat-of-arms and the Victorian crown painstakingly polished and pointing directly forward. Gleaming too were the numbers on his collars and the small white metal buttons on his jacket.

'You have a message for me, Constable,' Jarrett said softly.

'Yes, sir. From Inspector Grant. It's a body, sir. A probable murder.'

'Damn it!' It was the start of the Glasgow Fair. Originally for the sale of horses and cattle on the third and fourth week of July of every year, now it covered a vast area of the people's park known as the Glasgow Green, and included makeshift theatres, circuses and booths of all kinds, as well as street performers and social commentators. Through all of this wove an army of pick-pockets, whores and tricksters, all preying on the thousands of visitors from surrounding towns and villages. It was the worst possible time of the year to locate any one individual. 'Where?'

'Third railway arch on West Lane, sir. It's on my beat.'

'You found him?'

'Yes, sir. At six o'clock this morning.'

Baptism of fire, Jarrett thought. Yet the boy had to be broken in sooner or later, so it might as well be now.

'Did you come by wagon?' he asked.

'Yes, sir, it's waiting outside.'

'Then let's go. You can tell me everything *en route*.'

According to the young MacLean, there was no other indication of foul play beyond a small and relatively bloodless puncture in the chest, which obviously suggested an immediate cessation of the heart's action. The body, he said, had not been there at four o'clock, so assuming it hadn't been dumped it was reasonable to assume that the killing took place sometime between four and six. Although it is difficult to gauge height in the horizontal, the constable guessed that the victim was a little under six feet, slim of build and probably in his late thirties. Apart from the ubiquitous sideburns he was clean shaven. As far as the clothes were concerned, he was well enough dressed, though not a toff.

* * *

Chief Constable Rattray had visited the death scene, grumbled about a bit while satisfying himself that the deceased was not a member of any society he was part of, then instructed Inspector Grant to send for the superintendent and swiftly departed. Clearly, this was a simple disagreement, completely lacking the sexual interest of the Madeleine Smith affair or the gory butchery of the Jessie McLachlan case, so it was unlikely that the newspapers would be unduly interested. Put another way, there was little chance of publicity and even less hope of political praise in this sorry business.

The area around the covered corpse resembled a ploughed field. Charlie Grant crossed to meet Jarrett as he stepped from the wagon.

'Trodden to buggery,' he said. 'A bloody mess altogether.'

'Appointments,' Jarrett muttered, and Grant knew exactly what he meant. Neither of them had any time for those who had not risen through the ranks. 'Sometimes I wonder whose side he's on.'

'His own.'

The superintendent nodded, but it was plain that he wanted this topic to go no further. Criticizing superiors was a risky business, even when justified.

'Let me see,' he said.

Detective Sergeant Quinn drew back the

canvas as far as the man's middle. The coat had been opened to reveal the small wound and the limited extent of the bloodstain on his shirt. There was no waistcoat.

'Pockets are empty, Superintendent,' Quinn offered without being asked. 'The trouser pockets have been turned inside out.'

'Thorough job of thieving,' said Grant.

'Aye, too thorough.' The more Jarrett considered the scene the less he was convinced by it. 'Nobody steals handkerchiefs any more.'

'Maybe he didn't have one.'

'Oh, I think he almost certainly had.'

'Initialled, then. The killer might have tried to render him anonymous.'

'And exactly why would a random attacker want to do that?'

Grant shrugged.

'Neither of us really believes that this was a chance crime, Superintendent, do we?'

'What then?'

'Sudden quarrel. One stabs the other, then in his terror quickly removes all trace of identity.'

'Possible, I suppose. But what were they doing here at that time of the morning?'

'Returning from a drinking party?'

'No smell of alcohol on the corpse,' Sergeant Quinn said, then realized that he was perhaps talking out of turn. 'I mean, you would still be able to tell, wouldn't you, sir?'

'Yes, Quinn, you would,' Jarrett confirmed, then said to Inspector Grant, 'But we're guessing here. Has Dr Hamilton been alerted?'

'Rattray sent a cab for him to take him straight to the mortuary.' Grant nodded in the direction of the horsedrawn ambulance. 'Can they take him now?'

'Yes,' Jarrett said. 'Let's hear what Hamilton has to say.'

'Chances are he'll go along with us on the argument theory.'

'He might, but I don't like the wound.'

'What about it?' Grant asked.

'There isn't enough blood.'

* * *

Superintendent Jarrett had to kick his heels in the cool, white tiled hallway for the best part of an hour before Dr Hamilton completed his initial examination of the body and beckoned him into the mortuary proper. The body was on a marble slab, naked and covered only by a thin cotton sheet. A couple of yards away the clothing had been laid out on a scrubbed wooden table exactly as it would have been worn. Hamilton turned back the sheet just far enough to reveal the wound.

'Before we consider the fatal wound, Superintendent,' he said, 'I wonder whether you noticed the mark on his left cheek.'

'No, it was fairly dark in the arch.'

Hamilton placed his index finger on the point of the blow.

'Inflicted a short time before death. The bruise would be considerably darker had he lived longer.'

Jarrett nodded as he considered the implications of this.

'You say a short time. Exactly how short?'

'Exactly is not a word I care to use, Superintendent,' Hamilton said. 'A few minutes perhaps. Half an hour at most. I would assume that the killer struck him before finishing him off.'

But Jarrett was not convinced by this.

'No disrespect, Dr Hamilton,' he said, 'but it doesn't feel right. Whether it was an attack by a stranger or a quarrel between acquaintances, somehow there is too long a delay between the blow and the wounding.'

'You may well be right,' said Hamilton, moving his hand down to the puncture on the chest of the corpse. 'Not much to look at, but it was enough to put paid to this fellow.'

Jarrett leaned forward and took a close look at the small puncture. Most of the stabbings he had encountered in Hong Kong were messy affairs, usually delivered between the shoulder blades. By contrast this was almost delicate. Even allowing for the elasticity of the skin which almost always meant that the wound was slightly smaller than the section of the weapon, this still suggested a narrow blade of unusual design.

'Square?' he asked.

'Less than half an inch and possibly closer to three-eighths.' Doctor Hamilton rolled the corpse on to its right side. Most men would have found moving a dead body heavy going, but the Crimea had taught him how to use his muscles to advantage. The exit wound was even smaller. 'Not much more than an eighth of an inch.'

'No weapon I have ever come across,' said Jarrett. 'More like a tool of sorts.'

'Well, you have plenty to choose from, especially around here. Heaven knows what sort of gadgets they use in the shipyards or wagon builders. It might even be something the killer ground down himself in a workshop.' Doctor Hamilton let the remains sink back onto the slab. 'What about those brass knuckles a lot of the young toughs carry, Superintendent? You know, the ones where a spike unfolds.'

'That was my first thought when I saw the

wounds, but a knuckle spike isn't long enough to pass completely through the body. This object just made it and no more.'

'That being the case, I am going to have to leave that side of things to you. There was nothing in my war experiences that allow me to hazard a better guess. Give me the consequences of musket balls, sabre cuts and bayonet thrusts and I am in my element.'

'To each his own, I suppose,' Jarrett muttered, then asked 'What about a bayonet? They come in a variety of sections.'

'True — flat, round, square and triangular — but they tend to be long so that the entry and exit wounds are similar in size. This was a much shorter object, and it probably had some kind of round handle or hilt.' Hamilton placed the tip of his index finger on a slight, semi-circular mark around the wound. 'It is very faint, not much more than a dent in the skin, but that is because death was instantaneous. No bruising when the pump stops. If he had been fatally injured and managed to hang on for a time I think you would have seen a ring around the wound about the size of a shilling.'

'So we can say for sure that the blade was driven in to its very limit?'

'No question of it. One strike, thudded

home as far as it would go — end of story for this poor chap.'

On a change of tack, Jarrett said, 'Almost bloodless. What does that offer?'

'Only what I have already said. Sudden demise. Dead before he hit the ground.'

'An experienced killer?'

'Or a lucky one.'

'I was thinking more of an ex-soldier.'

'Well, there are thousands of former soldiers among the down-and-outs in every city in the land, and they all know how to kill.' Doctor Hamilton crossed to the wooden table and lifted one of the dead man's boots. 'What do you make of these?'

Jarrett took the boot, tested its pliability and took a good look at the soles.

'This was a man who knew how to look after his kit,' he stated after a few moments.

'Like a soldier?'

'Precisely. Except that you couldn't call him a down-and-out. Anything but.'

'Officer?'

'Perhaps.' The superintendent lifted each item in turn, but it was the shirt that initially interested him most. The stripes were too broad and the blue too deep for it to be considered tasteful. 'A bit odd, don't you think? Looks foreign.'

'Possibly, but I don't have a lot to do with

these things. I can't recall ever buying a shirt. I leave all that to the good wife.'

Jarrett laid the shirt back into place and asked, 'Anything else, Doctor, anything you can determine that might assist me?'

'There is no wedding ring and no sign of one having been worn.'

'Any more?'

Hamilton looked slightly sheepish. Even after a lifetime in the profession certain matters were still difficult to discuss.

'Well,' he said, hesitantly, 'even though he doesn't appear to have been married, he was with a woman shortly before he died.'

'With?'

'You know what I mean.'

'Not . . . ?'

'Precisely.'

'Can you be sure? What I mean is — ?'

'You may take my word for it, Superintendent. Our corpse had been, for the want of a better word, indulging in the pleasures of the flesh.'

'Perhaps he was married. Not everyone likes to wear a ring.'

'That's true. He may have had an early morning romp before setting off for work.'

'Do people actually behave like that?' Jarrett asked.

'So I'm told,' said Hamilton.

* * *

'A pimp,' Inspector Grant put forward when Jarrett returned to his office at the Central and called in Charlie Grant and young Tommy Quinn. 'There was a disagreement over money, or whatever, and the pimp stabbed him. Then, to make it worth his while, he took everything the victim had on him.'

Jarrett wrinkled his nose. He didn't like the theory very much, even though it was now the most obvious first choice, the presence of a female having consigned the swift falling out idea to the back burner. The time delay between the blow and the fatal strike still troubled him.

'It doesn't make sense,' he said. 'And there is something wrong with the weapon.'

'I would have said it was far from wrong, Superintendent. Did the job admirably.'

Jarrett had brought the man's clothes from the mortuary and the now untied parcel occupied the middle of his desk. Charlie Grant held up the trousers, the pockets of which still hung out like two dead wings from the sides of the garment. There had been no need to pull the lining out of the jacket pockets as they were sufficiently capacious to permit a quick rummage.

'Could have been a hold-up that went wrong,' he suggested. 'Maybe turned out his pockets himself, then suddenly decided to have a go.'

'Maybe anything,' Jarrett grumbled. 'It's all speculation. But it will no doubt come out in the wash. Right now, we need to know who he was and where he was from. I don't suppose anyone has reported a missing husband yet?'

'All the stations have been instructed to wire us the moment anything occurs,' Sergeant Quinn said. 'But I would have thought he was local.'

'Agreed. Instinct says that he probably lived within half a mile of where he was found. Whether it was a whore or a dalliance with a wife he couldn't actually lay claim to, there was no possible means by which he was going to travel any appreciable distance. The greater likelihood is that he both lived and worked within walking distance of the murder spot.'

'Of course,' Charlie Grant said, 'if he was single and in digs the landlady might never report his disappearance. A lot of them are used to fly-by-nights, so they just lay claim to any items left behind and rent out the room again.'

'I can't imagine Mrs Maitland behaving in

such a fashion,' Jarrett said.

'Perhaps not, Superintendent, but you couldn't describe yourself as being in digs.'

'Paying guest is the correct expression. Mrs Maitland's is a superior guesthouse.'

'Exactly so.' Grant winked at the young Irishman when he was sure Superintendent Jarrett's attention was elsewhere. Trouble with the superintendent was that you could never really be sure how he was going to take it. When he was relaxed he could laugh with the best of them, but when the pressure was on he might come back at you like a coiled snake. 'Now, do we wait for his absence to be logged, or are we off on the trudge?'

'We can't assume anyone will miss him. You take the suit, Inspector, and young Quinn here can take the boots.'

'That leaves the shirt, Superintendent,' Grant observed. 'Are you sure you can manage it?'

Jarrett rose from his seat and glared at the man, while Tommy Quinn studied the floor and stayed out of it.

'You are a disrespectful Highland rogue,' the superintendent stated. 'Twenty years in civilization and you still haven't learned how to address your superiors.'

'That's very true, Superintendent,' Grant

replied, 'but when you're too good to lose you can be that way.'

When they were out in the corridor, Grant with the folded suit in a canvas bag and Sergeant Quinn with the boots and socks in a small holdall, the young man from Dublin said, 'You're chancing your arm with the chief, Inspector. One of these days enough will be enough.'

'Not a hope. I know how far I can go.'

'Yes, but he gets a bit bristly when you mention his living accommodation.'

Grant laughed then, deep and soft. There was a coarseness in it.

'That's because he doesn't want anyone to know what he gets for afters,' he said.

Young Tommy Quinn blinked, momentarily confused, then he reddened from the collar up.

'You don't mean . . . '

'Listen, forget I said it. I've known Henry Jarrett since he came back from the Orient. We work well. And I think you're fitting in just nicely.'

'Thank you. Inspector.' At the start, when young Quinn first arrived, he had endured a great deal, and most of it from Charlie Grant. But he had shrugged and grinned and put up with it, because that was what the superintendent advised him to do. Now nobody called him 'Paddy' any more, or joked about potatoes, or even made rude remarks about the Pope. He had been tested to the limit and had come through with flying colours. Now that they knew he had stuffing and could be depended upon in a tight spot he had been accepted. 'How many bootmakers are there in Glasgow?'

'You're about to find out, laddie.'

'Unless of course I strike it lucky right away.'

'Life doesn't work like that,' Grant said and meant it.

2

It was the middle of the afternoon before Charlie Grant saw the first indication of a light at the end of the tunnel. Even then it was little more than a glimmer. Shimon Abelev's English was not good, but it was more than sufficient to make his point. The suit, he said, was in the Russian style. That was not to say that it was actually made in Russia, but the tailor was almost certainly Russian. The cloth, however, was a different matter. Mr Abelev had never seen it before and could not begin to guess at its origin. If nothing else, Inspector Grant, whether wisely or otherwise, promptly eliminated all non-Russian tailors from his Glasgow Directory.

Detective Sergeant Tommy Quinn, for his part, felt as though he was trying to cross a quicksand. The more tired he became the deeper he sank. Or at least his mood did. The boots had recently been soled and heeled, so it was probably more important to find who carried out this task than to actually find the original bootmaker. The often repeated suggestion that the work may have been carried out in another town did not exactly fill him with optimism. Then he arrived at Findlay's Boot and Bootee Emporium.

Horace Findlay, having been fetched from his office by a nervous salesman who had all but collapsed at the sight of the badge Quinn placed on the glass counter, scurried down the open-tread stairs and ushered the young detective into a small side room.

'Oh, yes,' Findlay said anxiously. 'That is our work. Is something wrong?'

'Not as far as you are concerned, Mr Findlay,' Quinn assured him. 'We are merely trying to identify the owner of the boots. Now, were they made in your establishment, or repaired here?'

'Both. We offer special rates to customers who bring our boots back for soling. We get a great deal of extra business that way.'

For the first time since he was called from his warm bed in Mrs Grogan's lodging-house by a burly constable whose knock could drive a door off its hinges, Tommy Quinn risked a modicum of hope. Only one tiny detail remained.

'Do you happen to know the name of the customer?' he asked cautiously.

'But of course.' Mr Findlay quickly drew out the lace from one of the boots and turned back the tongue. Almost at its very base was the number 6972 in pencil. 'If you will excuse me for a moment, Sergeant, I will check the ledger.'

The moment somehow stretched itself out to around five minutes, but the prospect of being the one who identified the murder victim made it more than sufferable. He whistled a little and occasionally hummed. Eventually Mr Findlay returned.

'There you are,' he said, handing Quinn a sheet from an order pad. 'George Sweeney, 23 Rowan Way.'

'I am greatly in your debt, Mr Findlay.'

'Say no more, young sir. Only too pleased to assist the police in any way I can.'

Although that kind of assurance would normally have caused the hair to stand up at the back of his head, Tommy Quinn was on this occasion too pleased with himself and the prospect of pipping his superiors to feel anything but elated.

Jarrett's day was much as he had expected it to be. Normally he would have delegated the slogging part of it to his assistants, but there were too many items and he had a sense of time running out. There was no good reason for this; it was just a notion that things were not as simple as they appeared at first glance. Whatever else it was, the killing was not a random attack by an opportunistic thug.

The shirt did nothing to quell his anxieties. After touring a dozen shops and getting absolutely nowhere, Jarrett caught a horse-bus and made his way to River Lane and the great red brick monstrosity that was the five-storey warehouse of MacKendrick & Steele, clothing importers and exporters. If they couldn't tell him about the garment, he had been assured by several retailers, nobody could.

Donald MacKendrick was a merchant of the old school. He knew his business and every bit of stock. Not for him a posh office somewhere up there in the clouds. He spent his days on the work floor, checking inward and outward consignments, making sure that deliveries and exports met their deadlines and, perhaps most important of all, ensuring that his loyal and respectful employees weren't thieving him blind.

MacKendrick spread the shirt out on a well-scarred and ink-blotched table. He could scarcely miss the hole caused by the weapon or the small disc of blood, now dry but not yet brown.

'This one isn't alive now,' he said flatly.

'I trust it doesn't upset you,' Jarrett offered.

'Hardly. I was at Sebastopol, Superintendent. I've seen them cut in half by cannon fire.' While he was talking his sharp eyes were darting here and there, making absolutely sure that nothing was surreptitiously making its way to Paddy's Market. 'Did you fight the Russkies, Superintendent?'

'No. Hong Kong Police.'

'Really? Cosy little billet. Well out of it.'

If MacKendrick hadn't been such a cheery soul Jarrett might have taken offence, but as it was he could only grin at the man's openness and audacity. Here was someone who had no fear of the police and very probably saw their role as protectors of his property against the filching tendencies of the great unwashed.

'The shirt, if you don't mind, Mr MacKendrick.'

The merchant lifted one cuff and toyed with the buttons. Then he considered the yoke. Finally, the side panels came in for close scrutiny.

'This is a workman's shirt,' he said at length. 'Double stitched and hard-wearing. You won't find its like on sale anywhere in Britain.'

The superintendent was confused but tried not to show it. A workman's hands were generally calloused and ingrained, but those of the victim were soft and his nails had received proper care.

'So you have never dealt in such garments?'

'I didn't say that. As a matter of fact I

exported two large consignments of these just a few weeks ago.'

'To?'

'The first was to Australia. Big demand in the opal fields, Superintendent.'

'And the other?'

'Canada. Have you ever heard of Barkerville?'

'To be perfectly honest, no.'

'Well you will, and it has all to do with gold.' MacKendrick nodded appreciatively. There were some words that just made him glow inside. 'First they found nuggets on the Fraser River. This led to a bit of a frenzy, so the British Government lost no time in creating the colony of British Columbia. That was just five years ago. Since then gold has been found in the Peace River, and now they're building the Caribou Wagon Road and a town called Barkerville, which they say is going to be the largest city to the west of Chicago and north of San Francisco.'

'And that is where you sent the shirts?' the Superintendent asked.

'Not exactly.' MacKendrick shook his head, smiling as though he couldn't quite believe his luck. 'I sent them to the headquarters of the construction company that was given the contract by the government. I understand they are at least partly owned by the Ship Bank.'

'Do you have their address so we can write to them?'

'Oh, I don't think that will be necessary. They are about five hundred yards away in Clyde Lane. Hunter, Duncan and MacLure.'

Jarrett mulled this over for a moment. 'So presumably the shirts were made here.'

'Not here or anywhere near it.' MacKendrick's eyes twinkled. He was laughing inside. 'Hong Kong, Superintendent.'

* * *

'Russian trousers and Chinese shirts,' Inspector Grant said, shaking his head. They had congregated once more in the superintendent's office to pool their findings and hopefully call it a day. 'Thank Christ the boots were made here. I thought this was supposed to be an industrial city.'

'Ships and trains,' Superintendent Jarrett reminded him. 'Not fashions for peacocks.'

'I wouldn't call the shirt fashionable,' Tommy Quinn said and laughed. 'I wouldn't be buried in it.'

'Well, this poor devil is going to have to be, if we can't put a name to him and find someone who is prepared to pay for his internment. I don't know what he aspired to in life, but it's a pauper's grave for all eternity.'

'Perhaps not.' Sergeant Quinn produced his trump card. He handed the order form to Jarrett. 'George Sweeney, 23 Rowan Way.'

'Well, bugger me!' Grant said. 'Talk about the luck of the Irish.'

'Not luck, Inspector. Brains and dogged determination.'

'My arse.'

Jarrett sank into his leather-padded chair and invited them to each pull up a chair. It was only right and proper, after all, since all three of them had been pounding the pavements for too many hours. He slapped the large brass bell at the side of his desk and a fresh-faced young uniform appeared in the doorway.

'Jump on an omnibus and make your way to 76, Delmont Avenue in the West End. Tell Mrs Maitland that Superintendent Jarrett will be late and that he wouldn't turn his nose up at a hotpot, if she would be good enough to keep it on the peep. You can draw your fare from the desk sergeant's cash box.' When the boy had once again disappeared from view, he said, 'George Sweeney. Wire the other stations, Sergeant, and see if he is known to us.'

'What about Chief Constable Rattray?'

Charlie Grant asked, when Tommy Quinn had set off for the telegraph room. 'He expressly stated that he wished to be kept informed about developments.'

'And he will be,' said Jarrett, 'just as soon as these details have been confirmed.'

'You mean let him stew in his own juices.'

The faintest glimmer of a smile seemed to form on the superintendent's lips, but it didn't last long and might even have been a trick of the light.

'I wouldn't quite put it that way, Inspector.'

'No, Superintendent, I know you wouldn't.'

The answer to Tommy Quinn's blanket enquiry was a resounding silence. George Sweeney, whatever else, had been a law-abiding citizen. Alternatively, he simply hadn't been caught at anything.

'Would you like me to follow up on the address, Superintendent?' Quinn asked, returning to his chair.

Jarrett shook his head grimly.

'No, I think this calls for sensitivity and tact,' he said. 'Inspector, you come with me. And if you have nothing better to do this evening, young Quinn, you might like to take a photographer down to the city mortuary and have a collodion plate made of our corpse. Face only, mind you, and as natural as circumstances permit.'

'But we've established the matter of identity, Superintendent, haven't we?'

'Let's say probably, but until Inspector Grant and I have located someone who will absolutely confirm it the possibility remains that your bootmaker has made a mistake. Personally, I hope you won't need a photograph, but to be perfectly blunt, Sergeant, it is safer to get the image on a plate before corruption begins.'

⋆ ⋆ ⋆

Rowan Way. Judging by the name it was probably once select, but was now grey and treeless between an iron foundry and the rope works. Number 23, like every other door in the street, was peeling and bleached, not as a consequence of the unrelenting sun, but through the corrosive action of an atmosphere laden with sulphuric acid.

The man who opened the door looked fifty but was probably in his mid-thirties. Greying hair and a drooping moustache has that effect. He looked at the gleaming badge, then at Jarrett and Grant in turn, then down at Grant's carpet-bag, his expression fixed and totally devoid of concern.

'Aye?' he said.

'A word, Mr . . . ?' Inspector Grant replied.

'Sweeney. George Sweeney. I've done no wrong.'

The detectives exchanged glances. This had not been expected. Yet they should have realized that young Quinn's lucky break would turn out to be less fortuitous than it at first appeared.

'Nobody said you had, Mr Sweeney,' Superintendent Jarrett said. 'It isn't about you.'

'Then you might as well come inside while I've still got a bit of my good name left.' He took them through the small lobby to the only room of any appreciable size in the property. The sleeping arrangements consisted of a large bed alcove with a thick curtain to keep out draughts. There was a small door beside the black grate, which Jarrett surmised led to wooden stairs leading up to a box room. It was a familiar pattern. 'This is the wife.'

Mrs Sweeney stood by the fire. She was a thin, not unattractive woman, with a small child in her arms. She nodded sullenly but didn't speak.

'Can I ask you to be brief?' Sweeney said. 'I'm on permanent nightshift and I'm due at the works in twenty minutes.'

'Where would that be, Mr Sweeney?' the superintendent enquired.

'Wilson and Atterbury. I'm a puddler.' Since it was clear that neither of them was any the wiser he added, 'I operate a ball furnace. We turn cast iron into wrought iron.'

'For shipbuilders?'

The man snorted. He was enjoying being smarter than the police.

'Not much use for wrought iron in the shipyards,' he said. 'We make gates, fences, lamp-posts and the like.'

Charlie Grant placed his carpet-bag on the table in the middle of the room, flipped the tongue out of the buckle and produced the boots.

'Are these yours, Mr Sweeney?'

The ironworker accepted the items and frowned at them.

'Aye,' he said. 'They're my best ones. Where the hell did you get them?'

'All in good time, sir.' Grant brought out the shirt which was folded to conceal the bloody tear. 'Recognize this?'

'Hartman wears something like that.' Sweeney glared at his wife. 'Did you give him my boots?'

The woman shook her head.

'No,' she said. 'He must have taken them.'

'We'll see about that.' Sweeney laid the boots by the fire and reached for his jacket which hung on a stout wooden peg. 'I'll have to go, or they'll dock me. I can't afford that.'

'Sorry, Mr Sweeney, but we're not finished.' Jarrett blocked the man's way when it was clear he was making for the door. 'Who exactly is Hartman?'

'William Hartman, the lodger. I don't like the man, but I need his money.'

'Do you know where he is right now?'

'Couldn't say. He leaves the house before I get home in the morning, so the only time I see him is at tea time, just before I go off on my shift. He's generally in before this, which means she's going to have to make him something.'

'Do you know where he works?'

'I have no idea.' By now, the puddler, as he termed himself, was getting impatient. 'Look, what's bloody well going on here? Is Hartman in trouble? What has he done?'

'Let me ask the questions, sir,' Jarrett said. 'Have you and Hartman ever quarrelled?'

'Not as such. We don't talk enough to quarrel.'

'What is your opinion of him?'

'He's a cocky bugger, but maybe they all are.'

'They?'

'Canadians. That's where he says he's from — Canada.'

'So what is he doing here?'

'Damned if I know.' Sweeney moved past

and this time the superintendent made no attempt to stop him. 'Now, either you're finished with me or you can make up the difference in my wages.'

When the ironworker had stormed off into the cool evening and the pots were still swinging on their hooks as a result of the slammed door, Jarrett said, 'If you don't mind, Mrs Sweeney, I would like to see Hartman's room.'

'Help yourself.' With her free hand she twisted the brass knob and swung open the small door. As expected the wooden stairs were narrow and the turn tight. She did not lead the way. 'Is he in trouble?'

'I'm afraid so,' Jarrett said as he passed her by and ducked under the beam. 'Perhaps you could answer a few questions my inspector has for you.'

Lodgers tend not to have many possessions, other than the few bits and pieces they can easily bundle together when it is time to move on. On the small table beside the single cot bed was a copy of the *Glasgow Post Office Directory, 1859–1860*. The same edition, in fact, that he, Grant and Quinn used almost daily. They were only brought out every four or five years, so this was the latest one available. Had Hartman been looking for work? It would appear that he already had some form of employment, but perhaps he was seeking to improve his lot. Or there may have been an entirely different reason for scouring the pages of the directory.

The superintendent got down on his knees for a perusal of whatever nestled beneath the bed. There was the usual pan, of course, and another pair of boots, well worn and with a split on the right sole. No wonder he had borrowed Sweeney's bests, but how long had this been going on for? It was extremely unlikely that Mrs Sweeney had not known of it, particularly as it was pretty obvious what had been going on between them while the puddler was making his wrought-iron gates. Pan and boots apart, there was nothing else of interest below the bed.

There was a small chest of drawers below the skylight window on the sloping roof. The top drawer held only a small bag with necessary toiletries, the middle one contained another shirt of the same type as the one he died in, and the bottom one was empty. There were no other clothes, no Bible, no letters from home, no pictures of a loved one far away and no samples of his handwriting. In short, there was nothing whatsoever to prove that William Hartman, late of Canada, had ever been here.

Mrs Sweeney still wore that same sullen

expression when Superintendent Jarrett came back down and closed the plank door behind him.

'Presumably Inspector Grant has told you about Hartman,' he said.

The woman nodded. Whatever had existed between her and the lodger was not sufficiently important for her to shed a tear.

'I'm not going to go to look at him in that place,' she said. 'You can't make me. And George won't go either.'

'Your husband will go where I tell him.' Jarrett closed in on her. 'As a matter of fact, he is the only suspect in the case, the only one with a good reason for killing Hartman.'

'What reason?'

'Oh, I think you know exactly what I mean, Mrs Sweeney. Your husband is no fool.'

'And no murderer, either.' Her eyes darted from one to the other. 'You'd be better employed looking for Lorimer.'

Jarrett narrowed his eyes and considered the woman for quite some time, while she sought to stare him out.

'Where did that name suddenly come from?' he asked. 'Did you just pull it out of the air?'

'No. He came here a couple of weeks ago to see Bill Hartman. The two of them were upstairs for a good hour or more.'

'Wasn't Hartman at work?'

'It was in the evening. I could hear him walking about up there while Lorimer was there. He was obviously very anxious about something.'

'Was it money? Did he owe this man something?'

The woman shrugged lightly.

'How do I know?' she said. 'He wouldn't tell me.'

'No, but that doesn't mean you didn't listen.' Before Mrs Sweeney could object, the superintendent added, 'I know these houses. That stairwell is as good as an ear trumpet.'

Since it was obvious that lying wasn't getting her anywhere, the woman said curtly, 'I didn't understand any of it. It was all nonsense to me.'

'What sort of nonsense?'

'I can't remember.'

'Well, I suggest you try harder, because I am going to haul your husband in for questioning and I intend to keep him in the cells until he confesses. If you can come up with some information that helps us find this Lorimer character then you'll get your husband back. If you can't . . . well, I don't need to find the weapon in order to hang him in Jail Square. As far as any jury in the land is concerned, a lodger having his way with a man's wife would be motive enough for murder.'

During this exchange, Charlie Grant had been prowling around the room, lifting this and looking behind that, but it wasn't until he ran his fingers along the dusty top of the old dresser that he found something of interest.

'What do you make of this, Superintendent?' he asked. 'Solid gold, by the feel of it.'

Jarrett took the offered watch and flicked open the case. The initials read W.H. The date was 1861.

'Care to tell me about this, Mrs Sweeney?' he asked coldly.

The woman stared at the hunter. She was thinking fast and furiously, but nothing substantial was coming.

'It's Bill's,' she whispered hoarsely.

'I deduced that much. What I want to know is how it got there.' He held it up in front of her eyes so that she would be in no doubt as to his sincerity. 'This watch could hang you both, Mrs Sweeney. Be under no illusions about that fact. Now tell me everything you know, or I'll place you under arrest right now.'

In the short time they had been in George Sweeney's house the July evening had lost its warmth and there was a distinct chill in the air. Jarrett and Grant climbed into the waiting police wagon and instructed the driver to set off for Wilson and Atterbury's works. Sweeney would just be starting work, perhaps for the last time in his miserable life.

3

George Sweeney was a great deal less sure of himself now that he was sitting in the interrogation room. He was sweating profusely and trying desperately to avoid catching Charlie Grant's eyes, but that was proving almost impossible. No matter how he turned his head the quickly darting inspector was always in front of his face. But he wasn't talking any more. He was yelling now because it was past eight o'clock and he wanted to get home.

'You walked in on them, didn't you, Sweeney?' Grant half-stated, half-demanded. 'Were you earlier than usual? Was he still lying on her tits?'

'No.' Sweeney looked at young Quinn, as though appealing for him to intervene. The younger man seemed more understanding somehow. 'I'm telling you the truth. It wasn't like that.'

'What was it like?' Charlie Grant asked loudly. 'If that wasn't the reason for it, what was?'

'The reason for what?'

'For killing William Hartman. Are you

stupid, Sweeney? Who do you think we've been talking about for the last two hours?'

'I didn't kill Hartman. How many times do I have to tell you that?'

Charlie Grant returned to the other side of the plain desk and sat glaring at the uncomfortable ironworker.

'You shouldn't have taken the watch, you know,' he said flatly. 'That'll hang you. They would be sympathetic if you caught him on the job and lost your head, but the watch puts an entirely different complexion on it. It suggests premeditated murder for profit.'

'And what about the rest of his stuff?' Sergeant Quinn asked suddenly after a prolonged period of silence. 'Where have you hidden that?'

'What stuff?' Sweeney squirmed in his chair and for the umpteenth time drove his calloused fingers through his thick hair. 'He didn't have any stuff.'

'You're lying!' Charlie Grant startled the suspect. 'There wasn't enough in his room to fill your cap. No man has that little to show for thirty-odd years of life.'

'Well, he had. When he wasn't working he was sleeping.'

'Yes, and we know who with, don't we?'

Sweeney stared at the inspector for some time, then said, 'You don't understand. It isn't what you think.'

Charlie Grant sat forward suddenly. He glanced at Tommy Quinn to see if he had picked up on that. He had.

'Are you saying it's true?' Grant asked, but he sounded almost human now. The last thing he wanted was for Sweeney to clam up now that he had started to loosen. 'Did you catch him stoking her fire?'

The ironworker nodded. His clasped hands were in turmoil now, as his rough fingers twisted this way and that.

'Yes,' he said softly. 'They didn't even have the decency to cover themselves with a sheet.'

'What did you do, Mr Sweeney?' Now Grant was adopting his civil approach, giving the man his due and proper title. 'I know what I would do.'

'Aye, and any man worth his salt. I dragged him off her and out of her.'

Sergeant Quinn had been leaning against the wall between two barred windows. He tried to look casual as he strolled across to the door, but it wasn't easy. This was his first murder case and it looked very much as though he was going to be in at the conclusion.

'Did you hit him?' Grant asked.

'Aye. What would you have done?'

'I'd have kicked six bells out of him.'

This answer seemed to reassure Sweeney. He was less anxious now. When the door opened and closed behind him for the second time in as many minutes, he glanced over his shoulder and saw that they had been joined by a higher power. Tommy Quinn returned to his place at the wall while Henry Jarrett took the chair Inspector Grant vacated for him.

'Proceed, Inspector,' Jarrett said. 'Pick up where you left off.'

Grant brought a stool from a corner beside the unlit fire and positioned himself at the end of the table, facing Quinn and between Jarrett and Sweeney.

'You admit that you hit Hartman when you caught him with Mrs Sweeney,' he said. Normally he would have said 'the tart' or 'the whore' but the last thing he wanted to do was antagonize the chicken. The fox would be in the henhouse soon enough and all pretence would be booted over the wall. 'How often did you hit him — once? More?'

'Just once. She got a hold of my arm and put an end to it.'

'And that was enough to calm you down, was it, Mr Sweeney?' said Superintendent Jarrett.

'Not calm, I'm never that. It's just that you get used to it.'

'So it wasn't the first time?'

'Nor the twenty-first.' Sweeney shrugged lightly. 'You've seen the way she looks. She can't keep her drawers up. I don't know why, but God made her that way.'

'Are you saying you caught her with Hartman before?'

'No, not him. He was just a spare prick as far as she's concerned.'

'Who then?'

'The lodger before Hartman and others.' Sweeney forced a laboured smile. 'How do you think we can sub-let a room in rented accommodation? The landlord gets his way every week, regular as clockwork.'

'Why isn't she laden with bairns like apples on a tree?'

'That's God's other trick: she can't have them. The child you saw with her was her sister's. She died bringing the unlucky little bugger into the world.'

'Unlucky?'

'Look around you. If he had been dealt a good hand he'd have died with her.' Sweeney snorted. 'But things aren't that rough for you lot. You're in the gents' pockets, aren't you? Especially you, Superintendent.'

'What exactly are you talking about?'

'I'm talking about your gaffer, Rattray.'

'The Chief Constable?'

'Aye. Comes down to the works in his

buggy. Fifty yards of the most ornate wrought-iron fencing, two gas lamp-posts and a couple of gates with his bloody monogram on them. All delivered and put up for him. And how much do you think that cost him? Damn all. It's all done with a wink and a nod. But if those directors get up to no good you and your laddies won't be allowed to get anywhere near them.'

Jarrett was clearly angry and finding it difficult to remain calm as he studied the man.

'Are you alleging corruption in the force?' he asked.

'Alleging? Your bum's out the window, man.' Sweeney leaned back in his seat, lulled into a false sense of security by being permitted to ramble. 'I don't know why I'm wasting my time telling you this. If you're his men you're probably tarred with the same brush.'

Ever mindful of his honesty and sense of fair play, young Quinn angrily pushed himself away from the wall but sank back again when Inspector Grant glared at him. For some unfathomable reason Sweeney appeared to think that he had said as much as he needed to and that he was getting away with it. But it wasn't going to be like that.

'Tell me about Lorimer,' Jarrett stated flatly.

Sweeney blinked, confused.

'Who?'

'Lorimer. He visited Hartman in your house a couple of weeks ago.'

'First I've bloody well heard of it.' Sweeney quickly glanced at each of the three faces. 'Is this some kind of trick? Am I supposed to say I've heard of this character just so you can say I'm a liar?'

'No,' Jarrett leaned back in the chair. It was true. Sweeney had never heard of this man and possibly for a very good reason. His wife made it up. Time to change tack. 'After you hit Hartman, did you follow him and kill him?'

Sweeney stared at him.

'How many times have I got to tell you lot: I've never killed anyone.'

'Where did you put the weapon?'

'What weapon?'

'Where is the rest of his gear?' Grant snapped, causing him to jump. 'And why did you conceal the watch up there? Did you think we wouldn't check it?'

'Come on, man,' Jarrett interrupted. 'You might as well get it over with.'

'I'm telling you, I never killed him and I didn't steal anything.'

'An honest man, are you? Don't get many of them in a dozen.'

'Do I have a record?' Sweeney leaned forward, because when you are trapped in a corner there is nowhere else to go. 'Come on, do I? Show me my record. I haven't got one. I have never even been charged with anything let alone convicted.'

'That just means you've never been caught,' Sergeant Quinn said.

'Doing what? Listen to me — '

'Where did you hide the weapon?' Jarrett repeated. 'We'll find it, you know. We'll take that house apart with a claw hammer until we do.'

'I don't have any weapons.'

'A tool, then. Is that what you used — a work tool?'

'I don't use tools. I've told you before, I'm a puddler. I make cast iron.'

'I repeat, why did you leave the gold watch on the top of the mantelpiece?' Grant snapped, rising quickly from his chair and peering closely into Sweeney's face. 'Come along, man. You're wasting our time and if I miss my tea because of you you'll really catch it.'

'You've no right to threaten me.'

'I'm not threatening you; I'm making you a promise. If you don't confess now I'm going to go and get my gardening boots and give you a right kicking.'

'Superintendent,' Sweeney pleaded, 'are you going to let him talk to me this way?'

'Yes,' Jarrett said honestly.

'You would let him kick me?'

'That's not the same thing at all,' Jarrett admitted. 'But I suppose he could do a lot of mischief in the time it takes me to go for a pee.'

'That isn't fair. I've never harmed anyone and you've got no reason to think I have.'

Jarrett ignored this and said, 'You know, leaving that watch where it could be found was an unforgivable act of stupidity. If you had put it away with the rest of the stuff we would have had no real cause to suspect you.'

'Listen,' Charlie Grant said, 'there's no reason for putting the boot in. Mrs Sweeney could sign a statement saying that Hartman lost the watch while he was forcing himself on to her, and that you naturally became so incensed when you discovered that he had ravished your wife that you pursued him through the streets and did him to death. A jury would certainly be sympathetic under those circumstances.'

But Sweeney wasn't about to be fooled that easily.

'I didn't kill him,' he said, shaking his head. 'I didn't steal his belongings and I didn't murder him.'

'Is that your final word?' Jarrett asked.

'Yes, I didn't do it, any of it.'

Henry Jarrett rose to his feet and flicked open his silver pocket watch.

'Nothing to be gained from running round and round the same track all night,' he said. 'Charge him with the murder of William Hartman, Inspector Grant.'

* * *

He was always around, watching the unlucky and the dregs being brought to the desk sergeant, forever looking for the story that would make all the difference. He must have been a born optimist, or he would have found something else to do a long time ago. He was Jimmy Lyle from the *Advertiser* and he enjoyed an uneasy relationship with the police.

He sidled over to the desk and rested on one elbow. At least Sergeant Black was human, which was more than he could say about the Detective Department.

'You'll be dropping in at the club on your way home, Davie,' he said casually. It was an offer of a drink or two, but couched that way it couldn't be construed as a bribe.

'Don't see why not.'

'Good.' Lyle slid his pad across. Davie

Black penned a brief note and slid it back. 'I'll see you then, man.'

It was still reasonably warm when he stepped out on to the pavement. And it was dry, which was unusual for the start of the Glasgow Fair. Traditionally it bucketed and folk had come to accept that because a holiday was a holiday, even if the rain was running down inside your collar and out of the arse of your trousers. At least that's how they usually described it, although he hadn't actually seen it in action. Still, he knew exactly what they meant.

It was straight to the point. George Sweeney, 23 Rowan Way. Charged with murder by stabbing.

* * *

Superintendent Jarrett's Wardian plant case was nicely gothic, as wide as the window recess in his room and standing sensibly waist-high on its iron base. Before purchasing it he had thought long about the different styles — side opening, front opening and top opening, and had eventually decided on top opening. While it was all purely arbitrary, he had convinced himself that this was the best and most convenient for planting and adornment.

Although essentially an enclosed world of ferns, designed to protect them from the ravages of the industrial city, the other features were of equal importance to him. At the centre of the base was a small pool of water, necessary to maintain the moist atmosphere, but which had to be regularly siphoned off and replaced were it not to stagnate. Several small lumps of old mortar-caked wall were placed here and there to give a sense of scale, as well as providing necessary lime, and a couple of larger examples were meant to represent pinnacles or volcanic cores. But the main inhabitants of the glazed case were the ferns themselves — oak fern, soft shield, hart's tongue and venus's hair were most in evidence, while a maidenhair spleenwort clinging like a limpet near the top of one of the pinnacles gave the impression of great height. As if to refute the allegation that he might be taking it all too seriously and thus be in danger of becoming a pteridomaniac — fern fanatic — he had added a little pottery man who fished forever in his own little pool. That flippant inclusion was just enough to separate him from the serious collector, for which he was eternally grateful.

Jarrett brought his cane chair close to the leaded glass case and set about losing himself in the lush green world. He had planted all of the ferns himself, of course, bar one. The tiny wall-rue on one of the mortar chunks had seemingly come out of nowhere, not as a result of the now discredited theory of spontaneous generation, but because the almost invisible spores were already present on the broken piece of wall. The conditions within the case were ideal for their development. Growing from spores is never easy, so it delighted him that in his ignorance he had provided just the right environment for it to happen.

Inevitably, the George Sweeney business leapt into his mind. Each time a file is closed certain details persist like an unwelcome aftertaste, until eventually replaced by a fresh set of problems. Only then does it fade, though never entirely. Sometimes doubt lingers.

With Sweeney it was primarily the gold watch. Why would a man like William Hartman hold on to an expensive timepiece when he was so far down on his luck that he had to borrow another man's boots? For that matter, what was a Canadian doing in cheap lodgings in Glasgow? In Henry Jarrett's experience young men seeking to better themselves headed westward from old Europe to the young world on the other side of the Atlantic. The only people from beyond the horizon he had ever encountered were in the various consuls around Blythswood Square, or were representatives of major companies. Hartman just didn't fit the picture.

Even though he had more or less dismissed the individual called Lorimer as a figment of Mrs Sweeney's panic-stricken imagination, Jarrett had to admit that she was very convincing. But many confirmed liars are. George Sweeney appeared to have no knowledge whatsoever of the man, and there was no good reason to suppose he was lying on that score. Was it conceivable that Lorimer could have visited the house without Mrs Sweeney even mentioning it to her husband? It didn't seem likely, which made his very existence questionable. Jarrett's immediate reaction had been to accuse Mrs Sweeney of pulling the name out of the air and nothing that had occurred since then had changed his mind. George Sweeney might not have been the world's best husband, but he was all that stood between her and the workhouse. Of course she would lie: she would say and do anything to keep his neck out of the hempen noose.

After considering the George Sweeney business for a few more minutes he decided that he was just inventing problems where none existed. There was really nothing much left to do and no particular reason for dwelling on it further. Sergeant Quinn and his team would find anything there was to find in the house, and even if the weapon wasn't uncovered and the rest of William Hartman's possessions were never located, the gold watch and Sweeney's admission that Hartman had been naked with Mrs Sweeney would be enough to convict him. In truth, Jarrett didn't care whether Sweeney swung or got life. All that mattered was the wrapping up of a case that had not been especially satisfying, so that they could move on to another that might be more so.

Whether it was by sub-conscious choice, or merely fortuitous, the little pottery fisherman bore an uncanny resemblance to Chief Constable Rattray. It had not been initially apparent, but one evening not long after he had set up his case the similarity suddenly struck him. It was all there — the grey hair and side-whiskers, the contrasting black beard and the pronounced Roman nose. Even the fishing pole looked like the CC's silver-topped cane, which he would use as a pointer, even to the extent of prodding junior officers on their chests while making a point. The only thing that was missing, in fact, was the silk topper and whatever it was that made an expression arrogant. Perhaps that comes from being a lawyer who leapfrogs into the upper echelons of the police without ever spending one moment on the beat. While Jarrett loathed Rattray and everything he stood for, he adored the little handmade ornament and admired greatly the creative ability of its maker. With little or no creative skills of his own, he could only marvel at the wonderful array of talent that existed in this world.

Then Sweeney was back in his thoughts. The weapon also troubled him. His first reaction on seeing the injury on the victim's bare chest was that this was a *Wu Jian*. During his time in Hong Kong he had come across a wide variety of killing tools, and this wound resembled those he had seen on numerous occasions. But on closer examination he could see that the hole was square rather than diamond-shaped. Wisely, perhaps, he had kept his theory to himself, because the exit wound on the man's back turned out to be quite simply too small — impossibly small, even for the lighter and smaller *Wen Jian*.

His next notion, which he also thought better of divulging, was that it might be a swordstick, but once again the difference between the entry and exit wounds ruled that out. Like bayonets, swordstick blades came in a variety of sections, from flat to round and square, but their length was such that the diminution of thickness over the depth of a human torso was slight. Even the shortest of bayonets did not taper to that extent.

Since the thing, whatever it was, probably now rested snugly in the deep silt at the bottom of the Clyde river — or ought to do if Sweeney had anything between his ears — further consideration of it was probably unnecessary. The findings of the police surgeon would be delivered to the Procurator Fiscal — there being no equivalent in Scotland to the English coroner — and he in turn would include the details in his decision to try Sweeney. Of course, the PF might decide that there was insufficient evidence to do so, and that would be his right. But the gold watch, the assumed and missing possessions, Mrs Sweeney's bed alcove activities and the absence of any other suspect or any other motive made it unlikely that Sweeney would walk free. This nobody, whose skin was cracked and brown from the heat of the furnaces, and who never had the luck since the day he was born, would attract a crowd of thousands and enjoy a brief moment of fame before they dropped him through the trapdoor to oblivion. Even then several minutes would probably elapse before he finally expired. Hardly worth it. But then it never was.

Jarrett crossed to the large brass bed and, having first removed his boots, lay down with his hands behind his head. His thoughts, as always when he stretched out on the thick feather mattress, turned to Elsie Maitland. It was never easy to keep an understanding private when there were servants in the house, and considerably more difficult if there were three other paying guests. However judiciously the oil-can be used, a spring interior always found a way of communicating the existence of an arrangement between parties. If that communication be rhythmic only the densest of the dense could fail to grasp the nature of that arrangement. Mrs Maitland, however, had something much better than a simple oil-can when it came to silencing the springs: it was called jealously guarding her good name and reputation.

Just over four years previously, Ernest Maitland, forty-five years of age, corn merchant by trade and glutton by choice, dropped dead on Argyle Street's broad pavement after a hearty dinner at the Scotia Club. He alone was surprised and that fact was written on his expression. He left his good lady wife in straits that were anything but dire, but Elsie was not one to use the capital if it could be avoided. She immediately turned 76 Delmont Avenue into a most desirable residence for single middle-class gentlemen.

Although she would scarcely admit it, she was no doubt hoping that one of those paying guests would make a suitable replacement for the man who worked and ate himself to death for her. From the outset, Superintendent Henry Jarrett and Elsie Maitland experienced a mutual attraction, but it was only recently that Jarrett, without so much as a by-your-leave, removed the small dedication plaque from the hallway wall and consigned Ernest Maitland to the midden at the foot of the garden. Assuming this to be a test of sorts, Elsie did not retrieve it or even comment upon it. That silent act of Jarrett's was accepted by both as the moment of commencement of their engagement.

Henry Jarrett was not a man to throw his money about. Over the years he had salted away a decent little retirement fund, fully intending to purchase or build a suitable property and, with a little bit of luck, find someone to share it with him. All the better, of course, if that someone had reserves of her own. Without actually asking her, he was now trying to decide whether it would be better to keep on Delmont Avenue — having booted out the rest of the paying gentlemen, of course — or sell up and move away from the city altogether.

But that would not be tomorrow. He had several years still to go before he could collect his pension and he had absolutely no intention of losing that by quitting early.

Suddenly, there was a soft rap on the door and he was instantly on his feet. Then it opened and Mrs Maitland slid silently into the room. But when Jarrett placed his hands on her hips she removed them and frowned.

'You're not going to like this, Henry,' she whispered. 'That young constable is down in the parlour again. He says it's urgent.'

4

Charlie Grant came forward quickly to meet the cab. The arrival of Superintendent Jarrett meant that he no longer had to take the brunt of Chief Constable Rattray's anger. He could think of a dozen places he would rather be than the dismal alley known as the Waterdyke, especially at ten o'clock at night.

'Briefly, Inspector,' Jarrett said softly.

'Right, sir. A second killing, identical to the first. It seems that somebody alerted the press very quickly, because they were hammering on the chief constable's door in the middle of a bloody dinner party, demanding to know if we had an innocent man in the cells. It's about as bad as it can get.'

Henry Jarrett looked beyond Grant to the angry CC behind whom a bunch of reporters were being restrained by a number of very capable uniforms.

'I'll see Rattray first,' he said. 'Better get it over with.'

The chief constable was barely able to contain himself.

'Just what the hell is going on, Jarrett?' he demanded, but stopped short of actually striking the man with his cane. Or at least trying to. It had been rumoured that the superintendent had acquired other skills in China apart from making tea. 'My wife and I were entertaining the Lord Provost and his good lady when these animals began banging on the door. I assure you it was nothing short of a siege. The ladies were quite terrified.'

'With respect, sir,' Jarrett said, 'I think you might be exaggerating.'

'Are you calling me a liar?'

'No, sir, I was merely pointing out that if you had really experienced a siege you would know the difference.'

'Yes, well, that's beside the point.' Rattray jabbed his cane in the direction of the covered corpse. Sergeant Quinn and Inspector Grant were standing by the body, waiting for the CC to stop wasting the superintendent's time. 'Question, is what are you going to do about this? Clearly, you have locked up an innocent man and now these scavenging dogs of hell are baying for blood.'

'I quite appreciate that, sir, but you are really going to have to let me get on with the job in hand.'

'And this Sweeney character?'

'That remains to be determined, sir.'

'But if he is not guilty you are going to have to let him go and be seen to do so.'

'Perhaps, but there is the small matter of the watch. Sweeney may not be Hartman's killer, but it is possible that he may have stolen the dead man's gold watch.'

Rattray shuffled a little and grumbled a lot.

'Look, bugger that, Jarrett,' he said after a few moments. 'This is the time for grand gestures, not piddling around with trifling offences. They want to see Sweeney emerging from the gaol a free man. Consider the watch to be compensation. That should cheer him up and perhaps soften his attitude towards you. After all, he could accuse you of anything.'

'Meaning, sir?'

'Did you strike him?'

'I never strike anyone, sir, unless they start it.'

'Grant, then. He has been known to take the shortcut.'

'No one laid a hand on Sweeney; I can assure you of that.'

When Jarrett finally broke away from the CC and joined Grant and Quinn at the death scene, the inspector said, 'Same everything, sir, right down to the empty pockets.'

'Let me see the wound.'

Sergeant Quinn opened the shirt just enough to expose the square entry hole. As before, there was very little blood.

'Where do we stand now, sir?' he asked.

'God alone knows.' Jarrett shook his head.

But if he was waiting for a suggestion from either of the other two he had a long wait ahead of him. 'Pack him off in the blood wagon so that Police Surgeon Hamilton can examine him. I don't expect his report will add anything to our fund of knowledge, but at least it will buy us time.'

* * *

Doctor Hamilton had, as with Hartman, removed the clothes from the body and laid them out in wearing order on the wooden table. Once again, the trouser pockets had been turned inside out.

'Thorough individual, your killer,' he said casually. 'Not a scrap or a match to be seen.'

'Ring? Jewellery?'

'Absolutely nothing, Superintendent.'

The entry wound was square and a little under half an inch in section. The exit wound was, of course, tiny: same weapon.

'I don't suppose he had recently been in close contact with a female?' Jarrett asked.

'Not this time, I'm afraid.'

'Can you read anything from the body? I need all the help I can get.'

'I'll be able to tell you what he ate last. You can compare it to Hartman when you get both reports.'

‘You see a connection between the victims?’

Hamilton looked pensive as he moved over to the clothing array.

‘Only the age and manner of death, Superintendent. Clearly, it is the same killer in both cases, but some positive link between the dead men would dispose of any idea that the murders were the work of an opportunist. The coincidence would be just too great.’ Hamilton lifted one of the man’s boots. Examined it briefly, then laid it down and considered the other one. After half a minute or so he said, ‘What have we here? It looks as though we may have found a nugget, figuratively speaking.’

The stitched insole had been slightly loosened at one side, apparently deliberately by the look of the cut stitches, and a fold of blue lined paper was tucked within.

‘Lady Dawn, Slanaighear, Isle of Mull.’ Henry Jarrett tapped the paper thoughtfully. ‘It looks as though our cadaver has been moving in higher circles.’

* * *

It was 1.22 a.m. Normally, any outstanding business would have been put aside until the morning, but the storm whipped up by the newspapers had frightened the powers so much that they feared for their positions. And when they were concerned they wanted the waters to be calmed now, not later.

'George Sweeney,' Superintendent Jarrett said flatly. The ironworker was standing before him in his office, flanked by Inspector Grant and Sergeant Quinn. Two uniformed officers stood by the door, waiting to escort him out to the greater world that lay beyond the baying pressmen. 'I am withdrawing the charge of murder against you and instruct you that you are free to go. If, however — '

'Are you going to take me home?' Sweeney demanded. 'It's your fault, so — '

'Don't interrupt!' Jarrett was in no mood to put up with Sweeney's arrogant sneer. 'If, as I was about to say, you make a false statement about your treatment to the press, whether for financial gain or any other reason, I am going to haul you right back in here and charge you with the theft of Hartman's gold watch. That would be good for five years hard labour. Do you understand?'

'I understand.' The derisive expression remained fixed. 'And I understand that you're doing me out of my rightful property. That watch is mine.'

'It belonged to William Hartman: you stole it.'

'You can't prove that. The initials might stand for anything.' Sweeney held out his hand, the fingers jerking impatiently. 'It's mine. Hand it over.'

Henry Jarrett lifted the gold hunter from his desk, toyed with it for a few moments, then laid it back down again.

'Lost property,' he said.

'What the hell . . . ?'

'I repeat, lost property. The authorities have three months to trace William Hartman's closest relatives. If they fail to do so in that time the watch goes to the finder. That is the law, Mr Sweeney. I trust you will abide by it.'

The ironworker was plainly less than delighted, but it was better than nothing. He let his arm drop by his side.

'I've got no choice,' he said. 'Not that I ever expect to see the damned thing.'

'You'll see it, if we can't trace the rightful claimant.'

Just before he departed with the constables for his free ride home, Sweeney said, 'What about my job? Being released is not the same as being innocent in some folks' eyes.'

'Your job is safe. The chief constable will make sure of that.'

Sweeney nodded thoughtfully, then disappeared out into the dark panelled hallway on his way to the cool night.

'He'll say anything,' Charlie Grant observed. 'If they offer him ten quid he'd sell his granny.'

'Nothing we can do about it. We can only hope that my bluff keeps his mouth shut.' Jarrett returned to his chair and gestured for the others to sit or stand as they wished. 'George Sweeney is history. I cannot under any circumstances see how he could possibly be linked to the latest killing.'

'Where does that leave us?' Charlie Grant wondered. 'It looks like two corpses, one common weapon and bugger all else.'

'Not entirely. We have Lady Dawn, Slanaighear, Isle of Mull. And we have Lorimer, whoever he is.'

'I thought you had dismissed him as an invention by Mrs Sweeney.'

'As long as her husband was the chief suspect I had, but I can't afford to be so dismissive now.' Jarrett slid the scrap of paper across to Tommy Quinn. 'Electric Telegraph job for you, Sergeant. Lady Dawn, Slanaighear, Isle of Mull. But be careful what you say. We may be dealing with the aristocracy, and I have offended the great and the good quite enough for the time being.'

When Quinn had drawn the office door behind him, Charlie Grant said, 'I suppose we'll be trudging round the shops with the clothes again in the morning.'

‘I can’t see any alternative, unless of course Sergeant Quinn’s famous Irish luck holds out.’

‘It’ll be the shops.’

The expression on Tommy Quinn’s face said it all when he returned ten or so minutes later.

‘Nothing to do with Mull, I’m afraid, sir,’ he said, returning the small sheet to Jarrett. ‘There is no one called Lady Dawn and Slanaighear is a very unlikely name for a property. The telegraph operator knows what he’s talking about and according to him Slanaighear means Saviour. By his reckoning we should be looking in the Ship’s Register for these things.’

Jarrett shrugged lightly. It was as good a guess as any.

‘All right,’ he said, ‘follow that line up first thing in the morning, then we’ll do our favourite walk. Do you want the boots again?’

Quinn grimaced. Charlie Grant was laughing at him.

‘Might as well, sir,’ he said grudgingly. ‘It was the boots that gave us our break last time.’

‘And a right lot of good it did us,’ Grant offered. ‘Dropped us in the bloody mire.’

* * *

When Henry Jarrett reached 76 Delmont Avenue it had just turned 3 a.m. Although this was not a common occurrence it had happened before and allowances were made for just such an eventuality. As the hoofs and iron-rimmed wheels drew to a halt on the heavy cobbles, Mrs Maitland rose from her comfortable chair in the kitchen and shook Lizzie the maid who was dozing in the rocker. Both were fully dressed and had resigned themselves to the fact that the superintendent would not be home until he was home. Or at least Elsie Maitland had. Lizzie had long since passed the exhausted, whinging stage when her limbs ached and her head bobbed, and had given herself up to sleep, albeit of a shallow nature.

Mrs Maitland had made a point of letting her other three gentlemen know that Superintendent Jarrett had been called away on urgent business. In doing this she was looking ahead to his reappearance some time during the night and adequately protecting herself from the sort of wild imaginings they might have. Single gentlemen, they do say, awaken in an unfortunate condition and with an extremely limited range of interests.

Henry Jarrett's immediate requirements were few. A cup of Ti Kuan Yin, a slice of cold pork pie, a nice warm bath and whatever sleep he could grab out of the five or so hours that remained before he returned to his desk. It wasn't much to ask, but it did mean quite a number of trips for poor Lizzie as she carried buckets of water from the boiler to the tub.

* * *

Breakfast was a solemn affair, with each of Mrs Maitland's four guests quietly and studiously attending to his victuals. Not even Mr Sweetman dared to rent the silence. The reason for this was plain for all to see on the front page of the *Herald*. Superintendent Jarrett had admitted that a mistake had been made in the William Hartman murder investigation, for which he accepted full responsibility and assured the concerned public that no effort would be spared in the pursuit of the killer. Surprisingly, George Sweeney had little to say, other than to thank the police for their courtesy and fair treatment.

By eight o'clock Jarrett was back in harness, but Charlie Grant and Tommy Quinn had beaten him to it and were nicely ensconced in the cane chairs in front of his desk.

'We got off lightly, Superintendent,' Grant offered, grinning. 'Hardly recognized you in the article.'

Jarrett gave him a dirty look, but somehow managed to keep his tongue between his teeth. At least for as long as it took to count to ten.

'Right,' he said, 'common features — two bodies, both male, very similar in age, killed with the same weapon and robbed thoroughly right down to the dust and lint in their pockets. Differences — Hartman had recently been in close contact with a female and the nameless one had a fold of paper in his boot. We have already established that what appeared to be a name and address written thereon is nothing of the sort, and Sergeant Quinn is now going to pursue the suggested line of enquiry, namely that these are ships. Any observations?'

'Mistaken identity?' Grant half-suggested. 'Hartman might have been killed in error.'

'Do you really think so?' Jarrett mulled this over. 'It's possible, I suppose, but it doesn't ring true. Hartman was stabbed a quarter of a mile away from his digs by someone who very probably knew his habits. We don't know the identity of the second victim, or where he resided, but once again it looks as though the killer was aware of his movements. When we do eventually identify the second corpse I have a feeling that we will find out that he was in the habit of taking a shortcut through the Waterdyke.'

'With respect, that doesn't rule out the possibility of a mistake.'

'I think it does. It takes time to familiarize yourself with another person's routine.'

'All right,' Grant conceded, 'perhaps it wasn't mistaken identity. Perhaps he fully intended to kill them both.'

'Motive?'

'Revenge? They were both carrying something of worth? They were members of a society or religion he disapproves of? They were blackmailing him so he decided to remove them for good?'

'Very well,' Jarrett said, raising a hand. 'There is no need to go any further. In your opinion there was a very real connection between the two victims.'

Before Charlie Grant could confirm this there was a soft rap on the door and a young constable showed part of his head. His expression suggested that he was unsure how he would be received and was revealing no more of himself than he absolutely had to.

'Excuse me, Superintendent,' he said. 'There is a lady at the desk.'

'And?' Jarrett demanded.

'She is reporting a missing lodger.'

⋆ ⋆ ⋆

Mrs Harriet Jane MacNiven was short, plump and Godfearing. The first two attributes were immediately apparent; the third was by her own admission. She accepted the chair vacated by Charlie Grant for her, while Tommy Quinn stood awkwardly by. Only Henry Jarrett rose briefly and quickly resumed his seat.

'It's quite unusual for a landlady to report a missing lodger, Mrs MacNiven,' Jarrett began. 'He must be extremely valuable.'

Mrs MacNiven laughed lightly.

'Yes, I suppose he must sound like a keepsake,' she said, 'but in truth he is the ideal lodger. Herbert Fenton is teetotal, undemanding and pays me every Friday evening at six o'clock precisely. I don't think I could ever replace him.'

'Could you describe this Mr Fenton?'

'Certainly. He is about your height, mid to late thirties, dark hair parted on the left, and doesn't smoke.' Mrs MacNiven frowned thoughtfully. 'Oh yes, he is a Canadian.'

There was a long silence, during which the plump lady looked from one to the other and plainly wondered what sin she had committed that could render such wordly men speechless.

'Canadian?' Jarrett said at length. 'You're sure?'

'Of course. A very mannerly young gentleman. Obeys my rules to the letter, you know. He has never once attempted to bring anyone home.'

'You mean women?'

'Or men. Mr Fenton is a very private person and not given to unnecessary frivolity.'

Since the good lady had come to the station on her own volition and was not in any sense of the word a suspect, Grant and Quinn stayed out of it and let the superintendent ask all the questions.

'Tell me about Herbert Fenton, Mrs MacNiven,' Jarrett continued. 'For example, where he works, what hobbies he might have, if any, and so forth.'

'Well,' the lady answered after a few moments reflection, 'I don't believe he does work, at least in the accepted sense of the word. He rarely talks about himself, you understand. But having said that I did happen upon a letter in a jacket I was taking to be cleaned. In case you think me a busybody, it is only right and proper to examine a garment for coins, keys, etc, before handing it in. You would be surprised how many people leave sharp objects in their pockets that would damage the material.'

'Quite a few, Mrs MacNiven,' Jarrett conceded, his patience stretching ever so slightly. 'The letter, if you don't mind.'

'Well, it was from an acquaintance of sorts, although it was scarcely couched in the warmest of terms. Cool rather than warm you might say, though certainly not cold. And brief. Yes, quite brief.'

'The contents, madam. Can you remember what they were? Better still, do you happen to know if the letter still exists?'

'I really have no idea, sir. It might still be among his belongings, few as they are. Whatever else you can say about Mr Fenton, you cannot accuse him of being acquisitive.'

'In that case the gist, if you will, madam.'

'Well, as far as I can recall, the writer was informing Mr Fenton that he had not yet received notification that the money was *en route*, with the result that they would have to struggle on as best they could in the meantime. He was also displeased with someone, I believe.'

'Do you know who sent this letter?'

'Not really, sir, it was merely initialled W.H.'

Jarrett had half-expected something like this ever since she had referred to her misplaced tenant as a Canadian. Nevertheless, when it did come it was still something of a shock.

'Does the name Lorimer mean anything to you?' he asked.

'Lorimer? No, I don't think so. In fact, I'm sure I never met anyone of that name.'

Jarrett didn't really expect an answer in the affirmative, but there had been a few surprises recently and anything was possible.

'Please allow me to put a few random names to you, madam,' he said, flipping open his notebook. Since both victims were Canadian, any reference to the Australian opal fields seemed irrelevant. 'Fraser River . . . British Columbia . . . Peace River . . . Caribou Wagon Road . . . Barkerville. Hunter, Duncan and MacLure. Did Mr Fenton ever mention any of them to you?'

'No, sir, I'm afraid they don't mean a thing. My late husband did have a cousin called Duncan, but that was a long time ago.'

Jarrett rose slowly and skirted his large desk, signifying that he had no more questions.

'I am now going to ask you to do me a great service, Mrs MacNiven,' he said. 'I really have no right and wouldn't impose upon you if it could be avoided, but we have an unidentified body in the mortuary — '

'And you would like me to take a look at it?' she interrupted chirpily. 'More than happy to oblige, sir, although I do hope it isn't Mr Fenton. Most difficult to replace, if you know what I mean.'

⋆ ⋆ ⋆

Confirmation that both victims were Canadian led Henry Jarrett to review his mental list of priorities. It seemed extremely likely that the men were in some sense connected to Hunter, Duncan and MacLure and the whole British Columbia goldfield business, although in what capacity remained to be seen. Freed now from having to trudge the shops in search of an identity, thanks to Mrs MacNiven, Inspector Grant could now head for the headquarters of the construction company and make the necessary enquiries. But first he had to be armed with the right tools.

'We have a collodion of Hartman,' Jarrett said after Sergeant Quinn had returned from escorting Mrs MacNiven to the mortuary, then seeing her home after confirming that the cadaver was indeed Herbert Fenton. 'If you could arrange for prints of Fenton Inspector Grant will take one of each to this company to see if anyone knows them, by whatever names they chose to use. While he is doing that, Sergeant, you can take the Fenton image around to Mrs Sweeney to see if he has ever been in touch with Hartman. And somehow or another I would like the Ships' Register in London checked for *Lady Dawn* and the rest. By the way, did you warn Mrs MacNiven that I would call round to examine Fenton's room and such possessions as he had?'

'I told her to expect you some time this afternoon, sir,' Quinn said, pausing at the door. 'I also advised her not to touch anything or tidy up, but I think we are probably too late. Mrs MacNiven is the sort of lady who would dust you if you stood still for more than a minute.'

5

Somewhere along the line, Superintendent Jarrett had been told that an avenue was a broad tree-lined approach, yet the pavements were too narrow and there was scarcely enough room for a sapling in the postage-stamp front gardens of Chadwick Avenue. The terrace itself was probably no more than twenty or thirty years old and each of the conjoined house-fronts on either side of this dainty thoroughfare was virtually identical to all the rest. Even the small rectangle of grass and the neat border of well-behaved flowers spoke of a single hand at work. Not the Creator in this instance, but a gardener who gave perhaps two or three hours of his time to each property per week and thus attended nicely to the whole of the avenue between Monday and Saturday.

Mrs MacNiven could not have been more delighted with herself when she presented Superintendent Jarrett with the letter. It had been waiting on the hall table for him, just as she had been waiting in the shadow of the heavy curtains.

'Poor Mr Fenton placed it under his

mattress,' she said chirpily. 'When I gave it back to him he seemed to think it was of no importance, yet instead of throwing it in the fire . . . '

'Can you remember when it arrived?' Jarrett asked.

'The middle of last week, as far as I remember. Mr Fenton didn't receive many letters, so it was something of an event. I called up to him that he had post and he rushed down immediately for it. He even had shaving soap on his face, which was very unusual for him. He was always so immaculate.'

'Did he seem pleased? Concerned?'

'Neither, really. Bewildered more than anything.'

Jarrett read and re-read the letter. Mrs MacNiven's recollection of its contents had been relatively accurate, particularly as she had probably not been expecting to have to call to mind a note that was none of her concern. But there were omissions and they may well have been the most important elements. Initials, for example.

H.F. Still no sign of the money, so we have to bite the bullet and just do our best. That is the trouble with this sort of situation. Out of sight, out of mind.

Despite my firm instructions to stay apart, T.L. called on me to find out if there had been any progress. The man's impatience is intolerable and I told him so.

W.H.

'I don't suppose you happen to know who T.L. is, Mrs MacNiven?' asked the superintendent. It would have saved an incredible amount of time and effort.

'Sorry,' she said. 'Nor W.H.'

'Oh, we already know who he is, madam.'

The plump little lady stared at him for a few moments.

'The way you put it, sir,' she breathed, 'suggests villainy. I mean, when the police say something like that it means that they are interested in the party.'

'At this stage, Mrs MacNiven,' Jarrett said, 'there is no suggestion of villainy on the part of either W.H. or H.F. Quite the contrary, I'm sorry to say. W.H., like Herbert Fenton, has been murdered.'

'Oh, good Lord.' The lady placed a podgy hand on her chest. 'And T.L? What of him?'

'That is my main concern right now. If T.L. does not turn out to be the killer, then we must find him before he becomes the third victim. My instinct tells me he has to be one or the other.' Superintendent Jarrett indicated the stairs. ‘Now, may I examine Mr Fenton’s room, madam?’

‘Yes, of course.’ Mrs MacNiven trotted up the stairs ahead of him at a surprising rate, all things considered. The door to Herbert Fenton’s neat and airy room was already wide open in anticipation of this important visit. ‘There is not a great deal to look at, sir. Mr Fenton was a frugal man and not given to unnecessary or frivolous possessions.’

‘A man after my own heart,’ Jarrett said, smiling. ‘How long had he been here?’

‘Just over seven months. Always paid a month in advance and left the choice of meals entirely up to me. Some paying guests can be very picky, you know, requiring this or that and settling for nothing less.’

‘Shocking,’ he said. ‘People can be a nuisance without even trying.’

‘Are you telling me? Why, the gentleman who was here before Mr Fenton thought he was in the Palm Court, what with his list of needs . . . ’

Mrs MacNiven and her story that threatened to have no end faded into a background hum as Henry Jarrett drew open one drawer after another, examined the contents and looked beneath the paper liners, before replacing the piles as neatly as a man might do. This being well short of the good lady’s standards, while she continued to talk so she also fixed.

Jarrett had half-expected to find the same sort of blue-striped shirts that William Hartman favoured, but the two spares in Fenton's top drawer were plain white. One of them had been kept for best, the other well used and mended. Since there was no sign of a bachelor's sewing box, he assumed that Mrs MacNiven had looked after him well.

There were three books on a shelf above the bed. One of them, perhaps not surprisingly, was the *Glasgow Directory*. The other two were Hugh MacDonald's *Rambles Around Glasgow* and a thin volume about the district of Grahamston, which even now was in the process of disappearing beneath the new railway station. Already, rumours abounded of shops, hotels and even whole streets still extant beneath the new level, so swiftly was the work being carried out. It was the stuff of legend and no doubt there would be much embellishment in the days and years to come. Indeed, it was one such tale that perhaps suggested a career in investigation by inflaming his natural curiosity. It was said that in the dim and distant past a forgotten race built a subterranean labyrinth between Rutherglen and Glasgow. A young Henry Jarrett and countless others spent every free hour searching for the entry to this underworld in the graveyard of the ancient Rutherglen church, where Blind Harry the poet claimed that False Menteith betrayed Wallace for gold.

Neither young Henry nor anyone else ever found it, but at least it kept him out of trouble.

Superintendent Jarrett flicked through the pages of MacDonald. Nothing. He did the same with the Grahamston volume. Still nothing. Finally he checked the Glasgow Directory and found a pawn ticket waiting happily for someone to come along and rescue it.

'I will have to take this, Mrs MacNiven,' he said. 'It may tell us something.'

'But of course,' said the lady warmly, but her eyes betrayed a certain sadness. 'I can't for the life of me imagine what Mr Fenton could be doing in a place like that.'

Jarrett put the ticket away in his waistcoat pocket.

'I see he had a copy of MacDonald's book,' he said. 'Was he fond of rambling?'

'I suppose you might say that,' Mrs MacNiven answered. 'Although I would describe it as a daily constitutional rather than an actual ramble. Unfortunately, a silver-topped cane he was very proud of was stolen a fortnight ago and thereafter he rarely ventured out.'

Since the pawnshop would undoubtedly be closed by now, Jarrett saw no good reason for not taking a leaf out of Grant and Quinn's book on how best to swing the lead, and calling a halt to the day's events. Mrs Maitland would, of course, be pleased that for once she did not have to conjure up a meal just for him at some ungodly hour, and poor Lizzie could be nothing but delighted at having an evening to herself to catch up on her *Servant's Magazine*.

⋆ ⋆ ⋆

Superintendent Jarrett was waiting in the doorway when Archibald Speirs, pawnbroker, arrived, accepted the ticket before even removing his coat and promptly disappeared into the maze of shelves and narrow passages that comprised a good two-thirds of the shop. He was back in a surprisingly short time with a long brown-paper parcel, fairly narrow overall but sufficiently chunky and irregular to make wrapping difficult.

'There you are, sir,' he said. 'That will be two pounds and fifteen shillings.'

'It won't, you know.' Jarrett slapped the polished wooden surface, then slid his hand away to reveal the brass badge. 'Murder enquiry. This will either be returned to you in the fullness of time or redeemed, whichever the court requires.'

The honest Mr Speirs, lighter now by one pledge, stared open-mouthed as the superintendent drew the door behind him and caused the bell to add insult to injury.

'Well, I don't think much of that,' he said loudly, but not excessively so.

* * *

Having settled himself nicely behind his large desk, Henry Jarrett let the others see the letter Hartman sent to Fenton, but kept his news for last.

'Proceed, Inspector,' he said, when Grant had grumbled himself into a comfortable position on the cane chair. 'Hunter, Duncan and MacLure, if you don't mind.'

'Bloody rubbish. They've never heard of either of the individuals and no one recognized the quarter plates, although there was a considerable amount of morbid interest when they realized they were corpses.'

'But this outfit is supposed to be the leading construction company for the British Columbia business.'

'Yes, and the dead men are Canadians.

What does that prove? We linked them with the company with no justification whatsoever.'

'Not quite,' Jarrett pointed out. 'The clothing supplier who imported the kind of striped shirt Hartman was wearing maintained that Hunter, Duncan and MacLure and an Australian mining group were the only people they supplied. So there has to be a connection, even if you didn't find it.'

'Not exactly, sir.' Sergeant Quinn drew a folded garment from his large inside pocket and laid it on the desk. It was a shirt, blue-striped and unused. 'Paddy's Market. Two bob, sir. Sorry.'

Jarrett stared at the offending item for a full minute, then leaned back and stared at the ceiling.

'Jesus Christ!' he boomed. 'What the hell is going on here?'

'We are farting around in circles,' Grant offered by way of solace. 'We made a bad link and we've lost good time over it.'

Jarrett nodded grimly. He couldn't fault the inspector's analysis.

'Sergeant Quinn,' he said softly, 'how have you been faring?'

'Well, I managed to wake Sweeney who is due out on nightshift in a few hours, so a good bit of fun was had by all on that account. But at least I know now that I am a useless Fenian and that my parents weren't married.'

'You didn't have to go all the way over there to find that out,' Grant said grinning. 'You only had to ask me, laddie.'

'Enough!' Henry Jarrett gestured for Quinn to continue.

'I'm afraid Mrs Sweeney didn't recognize Fenton, sir,' the Sergeant said. 'According to her, the man who called on Hartman had wire-rimmed glasses and was also balding, or receding, depending on how you want it. I would say she was telling the truth. Lorimer, whoever he is, really exists.'

Jarrett considered this briefly.

'She also said that he spoke the same way as Hartman, which presumably means he is a Canadian. Unfortunately at the time I thought she was lying to save her husband.'

'Even if Lorimer is Canadian, it doesn't necessarily prove anything,' Charlie Grant offered. 'We know that Hartman and Fenton had nothing to do with the construction company, which seems to suggest that there is no connection with British Columbia, gold mines, or any of that stuff. They just happen to be Canadians, but that doesn't mean that the other members of the gang have to be.'

'Gang?' Jarrett looked confused. 'What gang?'

Grant shrugged.

'It's how I read it,' he said. 'They appear to be waiting for a shipment of money. That suggests only one thing to me.'

'Might be the way of it, sir,' Tommy Quinn offered. 'It isn't exactly a normal sounding letter.'

'If they did have a robbery in mind, what went wrong?'

'A falling out of thieves?' this from Charlie Grant.

'Before the crime? I hardly think so, Inspector.'

'It would make sense if Lorimer betrayed the others. Maybe they had served their purpose and there was no longer any need to split the proceeds three ways.'

'Not impossible, I suppose.' Jarrett gave this some thought, but wasn't overly keen on it. It just didn't sound right. 'So where do *Lady Dawn* and the other vessels fit into it?'

'They don't, sir.' Quinn handed over the Electric Telegraph message he had stuffed into his pocket when he returned from annoying the Sweeneys. 'No ships under those names. That's official from Lloyd's.'

'It gets better by the minute.' Jarrett reached down and presented them for the first time with the long parcel he had obtained from the good Mr Speirs. 'Let's see what you can make of this.'

With the brown paper removed and consigned to the waste paper basket, the contents seemed at first glance to be disconnected. There was a brass and leather telescope, which was under a foot long in its collapsed state, and a gentleman's cane with a silver pommel and a cheaper metal ferrule at the other end.

Jarrett extended the scope to its maximum, which was approximately two feet in length with all three draw tubes extended. He placed it again beside the cane, then he sat back and invited comments.

'It's a telescope,' Charlie Grant said flatly. 'And a cane.'

'Any street urchin could tell me that.' Jarrett frowned at him, though it was quite clear that the inspector was, as they say, taking a loan of him. 'Sergeant Quinn?'

Tommy Quinn lifted the telescope, looked closely at the maker's stamp, noted the name Kahler, satisfied himself that it opened and closed with ease, then raised it to his eye and peered out through the large sash window at everything in general and nothing in particular.

'Pin sharp.' Quinn was impressed. 'This is

scarcely a toy, sir.'

'Anything but.'

'A very nice piece of work, sir' he said at length. 'Fenton pawned this?'

'That and the cane.'

Quinn returned the now collapsed 'scope to the desk and lifted the cane. The pommel was fairly unusual, being a griffin's head, but then he wasn't exactly an expert on gentlemen's accoutrements.

'Didn't Mrs MacNiven say that Fenton's cane had been stolen?' He asked.

'She did indeed. Evidently her precious lodger didn't care to admit what had really happened to it.'

Quinn turned the object this way and that.

'Am I looking for something in particular, sir?' he enquired.

'Try the pommel,' Jarrett said.

'Sir?'

'Unscrew it.'

When the silver pommel was loose and laid aside, the exposed bolt immediately suggested a connection with the telescope mount. Without further prompting Quinn picked up the telescope and quickly screwed the cane into place.

'Am I wrong, sir?' he asked. 'Is this it?'

'It's called a monopod, Sergeant.' Jarrett turned his attention to Charlie Grant. 'Inspector?'

'Ideal for short-term observation,' Grant said, more serious now. 'Not as solid as a tripod but a good support for a few minutes. My guess is that Fenton was watching for something, but didn't want the world knowing what it was. I can imagine him setting off each day with his telescope in his pocket and his fake cane in his gloved hand, looking for all the world like a toff on his constitutional.'

'Agreed, but observing what?'

'That is the question, Superintendent.'

'There is another question,' Tommy Quinn suggested. 'If he needed it, why pawn it?'

'Either he was desperate for money, or he had completed his observation.'

'The latter,' said Charlie Grant. 'He wouldn't have pawned it if he still required it. He would have found money some other way, any other way.'

'Precisely,' Henry Jarrett said, nodding. 'But why would a man with worn boots resist pawning his gold watch?'

'Hartman, you mean? Perhaps it had sentimental value.'

'I don't see any sentiment,' the superintendent said flatly. 'It isn't as though the watch was a service award or a family gift.

Jarrett opened his top drawer, fetched out the gold hunter and laid it on the desk beside the silver griffin's head. Tommy Quinn, for his part, unscrewed the telescope from the cane and made up the set.

'Quite an assortment,' said Charlie Grant.

'Any ideas?' Jarrett asked.

Nobody had.

* * *

Mortuary attendant Hugh Breen snapped quickly out of his gentle dozing at the first sound of footsteps out there in the long corridor. He rose from his chair, drew open his cubicle door and emerged, mop in hand, to find out who had disturbed his reverie. The newcomer was thin, taller than average, and on the way to being bald. The eyes that considered Breen through the wire-rimmed spectacles were bright and piercing.

'I am looking for my cousin,' he said softly. 'Like me, he is on a visit from Canada, but it is possible that he may have wound up in this sad place.'

Attendant Breen laid aside the mop he had been pretending to use and adopted his most funereal expression. There was a time for dead jokes and a time for sobriety.

'Could you describe the gentleman?'

'About my age and generally average, I would say.'

'We have two such unfortunates,' Breen said. 'If you would kindly follow me.'

Their combined footsteps echoed and re-echoed down the long tiled passage. Eventually they reached what was known as the waiting-room. Not a place where visitors might rest, but a cold, small windowed, north-facing chamber into which the sun never shone and corruption was held at bay for a little longer than might otherwise have been the case. The Romans made ice in places like this.

Breen turned back the cloth on the nearest corpse just enough to expose the face. The tall man gave a little shake of the head. He then revealed the second face and again received a negative response.

'You have given me hope,' said the man, pressing a halfcrown into Breen's waiting palm. 'Perhaps my cousin is still alive and waiting to be found.'

Then he retraced his steps down the white corridor, pushed open the frosted glass door and was gone.

6

There was no love lost between Edgar Trimmer, bookseller, and any of his fellow guests in Mrs Maitland's establishment. He disliked the travelling salesman, Albert Sweetman, because he had a pasted-on smile and told jokes, something Trimmer was never able to do. He also loathed James Croall, the young assistant bank manager and greatly envied him his prospects. But most of all, and not without good reason, he hated and feared Detective Superintendent Henry Jarrett. Many booksellers did a good trade in what was known as Gentlemen's Art photographs, but Trimmer had taken it much further than that. He had his own photographic equipment and darkroom, and there was no shortage of hungry young girls who, for a shilling or so, would comply with his twisted requirements.

Regular toffs in search of something fresh, or in need of stimulation, knew better than to ask for the key to the cabinet. That was handed to them as a matter of course. Beyond the beaded curtain at the end of the long shop lay a small back room and the best selection of half-plate prints in the city. They were stacked on their sides in strawboard boxes, most recent at the front, so that the gentlemen could quickly and easily make their choice, then return the boxes to the cabinet and the key to the proprietor. They were fully trusted of course. People of that calibre would never dream of stealing.

It was the unknown ones who gave Trimmer the twitches and more than a few grey hairs. They would come to the counter and ask discreetly about the possibility of obtaining unusual photographic studies, without of course being in any way being specific in their requirements. At such moments he would have to make a snap decision, and this was usually based upon the age and height of the enquirer, and whether or not he had a regulation haircut. There was as yet no designated department dealing with such matters, but one or two recent minor tragedies among lesser booksellers had led to humiliating court appearances and evidence given by Sergeant Quinn. And he, it was known, was one of Jarrett's men.

On that particular day, Trimmer had more to think about than a possible first offence appearance and a shameful couple of column inches in the *Advertiser*. Jarrett, Sweetman and Croall were out and about, or otherwise attending to whatever it was they did, and Mrs Maitland was off by horse-bus through Eglinton to Pollockshaws on one of her occasional visits to her old friend, Daisy Sinclair. As for himself, he had taken a calculated risk and left the fate of the shop in the hands of his assistant, McCracken, with firm instructions that only regulars should be given the wicked key and everyone else flatly rejected, preferably with a thoroughly offended, holier-than-thou expression.

That left only Lizzie the maid and himself in 76 Delmont Avenue. It was a situation that suited him perfectly. He had designs on Miss Elizabeth Gill.

* * *

Although no more than an hour had passed since Harriet MacNiven placed her notice in the front parlour window, there came already a soft but distinct rapping on the outside door. This sent her scurrying in a manner that belied her plumpness to greet the newcomer.

Like her late and much lamented lodger, Mr Fenton, this stranger was also Canadian. He hovered over her and peered through wire-rimmed spectacles while giving her an appropriately pained smile.

'Herbert spoke so highly of you, madam,'

he whispered, 'that I felt that I must call upon you and thank you for your kindness.'

Mrs MacNiven experienced a mixture of delight at the compliment and disappointment at this not being a prospective lodger after all. Before she quite knew it he had joined her in the hallway and she found herself closing the door to the outside world, even if she wasn't sure why.

'Mr . . . ?'

'Lorimer,' he said, 'Thaddeus Lorimer.'

'Mr Lorimer,' Harriet commiserated, 'I cannot begin to tell you how sad I feel at the loss of your cousin. Mr Fenton was such a kind, dear man.'

'Indeed he was, madam. Popular with all who knew him.'

Mrs MacNiven smiled and nodded and wondered just exactly what to say next.

'Well,' she began, but only because she had to start somewhere, 'it is very nice of you to — '

'Forgive me, madam. I have, as they say, put you in a bit of a spot,' Lorimer said quickly. 'In truth, I was wondering if you could possibly let me see Herbert's room. As it was his last abode on earth I would deem it a great favour if you could give me a few minutes to commune with the surroundings.'

Harriet MacNiven brightened immediately

and came dangerously close to seizing his arm.

'Oh, Mr Lorimer,' she whispered loudly, 'may I take it that you are a believer?'

'In survival, madam? Yes, I must confess I am, although one should be cautious about admitting such a thing for fear of mockery.'

'You scarcely have to tell that to me, sir.' Without fully realizing it, Harriet was leading him up the stairs to the narrow landing. The door to Herbert Fenton's room was wide open and had been since Superintendent Jarrett examined it. 'Please, Mr Lorimer, take your time. I will go and make some tea. You do take tea, do you not?'

'Every civilized person does, madam,' he replied in his kindly way.

She paused briefly at the door and said, 'My dear Angus passed away nine years ago. He fell under a runaway brewer's dray.'

'I have always understood that horses will not step on human beings if they can possibly avoid it.'

'So I believe, but unfortunately the same cannot be said of iron-rimmed wheels and half a ton of beer kegs.' She gave him a half-sad smile. 'It isn't often that drink kills a teetotaller.'

Mrs MacNiven returned to the kitchen where she had been in the process of making tea for herself and discovered that the kettle was only now coming to the boil. She fetched her best china set, removed the kettle from the hob, poured just enough into the teapot to warm it, then emptied the latter again and spooned in three large measures of tea. Upstairs, the polite Mr Lorimer did not seem to be lost in contemplation. In fact he appeared to be moving things around.

She went on tiptoes to the foot of the stairs and listened for a full minute, then cautiously climbed the stairs and discovered that the door was now closed. Had silence prevailed she would have respected the gentleman's privacy and refrained from entering, but this was most certainly not the case. She had moved beds and rolled back carpets often enough to know what it sounded like.

Mr Lorimer was kneeling in the middle of the now bare floor. A length of tongue-and-groove floorboard was propped against the upended bed and he was reaching deep into the dusty recesses between the joists. When Harriet MacNiven appeared in the doorway without warning the thin man leapt to his feet and lunged at her.

The last thing she saw was a gloved hand fast approaching her face, then awareness deserted her in favour of oblivion.

* * *

'According to Mrs MacNiven,' Jarrett reminded them, 'Herbert Fenton's daily walk lasted about two hours. Now, if Inspector Grant is correct and he was watching something, how far could he have travelled from Chadwick Avenue?'

'He may have jumped on an omnibus,' Charlie Grant observed by way of a spoiler.

'That being the case, there is absolutely no possibility of finding out where he was watching from.'

'Not necessarily, sir,' Tommy Quinn offered. 'He could only have gone twice as far by horse-bus as he could on foot, and sometimes not even that. You know what sort of bottle-necks you can get into when all the delivery wagons are out and about.'

'Good point. Sometimes it's quicker getting off and walking.'

'There is also the expense, sir. I'm not sure that either Fenton or Hartman could afford to go by omnibus every day.'

'Clever boy, this,' said Charlie Grant, grinning at his superior. 'I mean, you only travel on the Menzies' bus because you can stick in an expenses chit.'

While Sergeant Quinn looked decidedly awkward and wished that the inspector wouldn't talk like that, Henry Jarrett glared at

Grant in an attempt to make him lose the grin. It didn't work.

'True,' the superintendent admitted, 'but at least it is an honest chit.'

'Meaning, sir?'

'Meaning that some people push their luck.'

'Disgraceful. Shouldn't be allowed.' Charlie Grant shook his head. 'You were saying, sir?'

'I was suggesting that we might be able to pinpoint his daily destination by calculating how far he went and how long he spent there.'

'That's hardly possible, Superintendent.'

'Even roughly.'

'Very well, we can try various possibilities. He might have spent half an hour walking there, an hour watching whatever he was watching, and half an hour back home again.'

'A good start, but I think it was you who said that the monopod was ideal for short-term observation.'

'I think you're right. It was me.'

'So we can safely say that this particular arrangement of telescope and single support lends itself to a watching time of five minutes? Ten minutes?'

'That depends,' Quinn put forward. 'How do you envisage him using it?'

'Meaning?'

‘If he was standing I doubt if he could put up with it for more than a minute or two. Play havoc with the lumbar region.’

‘Excellent. So he was sitting.’

‘Well, he didn’t have a collapsible stool with him, or at least Mrs MacNiven didn’t mention one, so it must have been something like a park bench.

‘Better by the minute. Grant?’

‘Bench, yes, park no. Unless he was watching the ladies in the hope that their dresses would blow up in the wind.’

‘Somehow I think it may have been a wee bit more important than that.’

‘I was merely trying to say that parks would provide limited opportunity for using a telescope. Generally they are too flat. What we are looking for is an elevated vantage point.’

‘Some parks have a high point, a seated observation area where they often put the flagpole.’

‘Then perhaps we should see what falls into a reasonable radius.’ Grant nodded happily as if agreeing with himself. ‘Allow one hour walking time each way and no watching time at all and that is our maximum circle.’

‘I will go along with that.’ Jarrett turned his attention to Tommy Quinn. ‘Any objections, Sergeant?’

'None at all, sir. Best to have a catchment area that is too large rather than too small.'

'And are we agreed that a gent with a cane could strut out, say, two miles in one hour?'

Charlie Grant wasn't entirely sure and was giving it some thought when there was a knock at the door and the young constable who drew the short straw entered.

'Excuse me, Superintendent . . . ' he began.

'One moment. How far can a man walk in one hour, son?'

'Three miles, sir.'

'Are you sure of that?'

'I do it every morning, sir.'

'Very good, lad, very good. Now, what was it?'

'There's a wee boy at the desk, sir. He says that Mrs MacNiven has been attacked.'

* * *

Lizzie Gill had never felt safe when Trimmer was about. There was something extremely unsettling about the man, and it wasn't only his resemblance to the Grim Reaper. More than anything, it was his habit of leering at her when there was no one else in the vicinity. If she ever found herself alone with him, she instinctively knew, he would almost certainly force himself upon her. Unfortunately, she was alone with him now.

She was sitting in the kitchen, beside the black grate, wondering how many times he was going to call down to her before he finally gave up. She wondered, too, what Mrs Maitland was going to say when Trimmer told her that the girl had ignored him completely and refused to provide him with a midday meal. What was she, Lizzie Gill, going to use as an excuse? How could she possibly convey her fears to the lady of the house without sounding foolish and immature? For that matter, did Mrs Maitland care in the slightest about her dreads and concerns? More than likely she would berate her for succumbing to her fantasies, and might even throw her out and replace her with someone less prone to nervous imaginings.

It would be at least four hours until Mrs Maitland returned from her visit to Mrs Sinclair in Pollockshaws, and considerably more than that before the first of the other gentlemen put in an appearance. It was inconceivable that she could possibly remain in her corner for so long and ignore the flat, monotone voice that repeated her name over and over again. There was no anger in the sound and that made it even more terrifying. It was the calm, endless, matter-of-fact repetition of that one word which chilled her blood and brought her close to screaming.

Finally, she got to her feet and stood by the well-scrubbed table for a further three or four minutes, just listening to her name echoing throughout the empty house. Without quite realizing what she was doing she reached out and selected one of the knives from the rack. It was just small enough to fit into the pocket of her uniform.

Every tread of the thickly carpeted stair felt like the climb to the gallows as it took her closer to the one who was taunting her. On the upper landing she again paused, but this time only briefly, before summoning up all of her reserves and approaching the only door that lay open.

Edgar Trimmer was seated in a buttoned chair, his thin, talon-like fingers gripping the padded arms as though preparing to launch himself forward in pursuit of his prey.

'Where are they?' he asked in that same unsettling tone.

Lizzie frowned and tried to make sense of this.

'They?'

'Where are they?'

'I'm sorry,' she said. 'I don't know what you mean, sir.'

Trimmer extended one long finger. It was

pointing at her pocket where an inch and a half or so of bright steel was protruding through the coarse cloth.

'Explain that,' he said.

She carefully took out the knife and laid it on the small table by her side. The idea of it made her feel silly now, almost childish. Worse, she was going to have to repair the cloth and hope that Mrs Maitland didn't get her eye on it.

'I was peeling apples,' she lied. It was feeble and unconvincing.

Trimmer continued to stare at her.

'Where are they?' he repeated.

'Please, sir, I don't understand,' Lizzie said desperately.

But that wasn't strictly true. Even before he said it she knew what was coming. It was every servant's dread, because there was no defence because no one would take their side.

'Three sovereigns, girl.' Trimmer indicated the ledge below the window on which lay a few worn copper coins, several new bronze ones and a couple of bright shillings. 'They were there when I went to the privy, now they're gone.'

Even though it was a lie and both of them knew it, all Trimmer had to do was keep up the pretence and she was in trouble.

'I never touched any sovereigns, sir,' she

said, her voice firmer now because she was trapped and had nothing left to lose. 'You know that as well as I do, sir. You know I never stole your money.'

'I know what will happen to you if I say you did.' Trimmer grinned at her for the first time. She preferred him as he had been. 'This isn't the first time, is it, Lizzie? You were dismissed before for stealing and were very lucky to find someone as kind-hearted as Mrs Maitland. Most girls would have wound up on the streets.'

'Mrs Maitland knows I didn't do it,' she countered. 'When I told her what had happened she understood everything.'

'Perhaps, but Mrs Maitland won't be on your side this time, girl. Superintendent Jarrett and I are close friends, and you know what a stickler he is for law and order. To Henry Jarrett there are few rogues more despicable than a servant who would take advantage of the trust that had been placed in her.' Trimmer rose slowly from his chair and beckoned her forward. 'You know as well as I do that Mrs Maitland and Henry Jarrett are more than friends. If she had to choose between him and you there can only be one outcome. And remember, they still send felons to Australia, although you will probably get off with a few years' hard labour if you look pathetic enough.'

Lizzie could think of nothing more to say, nothing at all that could possibly make him admit that he was lying. She watched helplessly as he fetched a box from the top of his wardrobe, placed it on his small desk and opened the lid with great reverence. It was almost like watching a religious ceremony being enacted.

First, there was a mahogany half-plate camera with a large brass lens. Trimmer set this aside and produced six plate holders which were also lovingly laid on the green leather surface. He then returned the box to its holy place on high and brought down a tripod. This he proceeded to extend while still grinning at her.

'Don't pretend to be innocent, girl,' he said. 'You know what this is and what it's for.'

'No.' Lizzie shook her head. 'It isn't right and proper.'

'Would you prefer to take your chances with Superintendent Jarrett? The choice is yours entirely, but if you choose wrongly there is no way back. Mrs Maitland will dismiss you and Jarrett will arrest you. There won't be one person in all the world on your side.'

After a few moments of panic-stricken thought, Lizzie said, 'They won't find anything, because I don't have them.'

'You've had plenty of time to slip out of the house and put them somewhere. Maybe that is why you didn't come when I called. Maybe you were out hiding the sovereigns.' Trimmer closed in on her and grinned into her face. 'I will also say that this isn't the first time. Little things have been going missing, but I overlooked them because I didn't want to get you into trouble. Now you've gone too far. Three pounds is a lot of money. I can't afford to lose that, so there was nothing I could do but report it.'

'I could go to Mrs Maitland about this,' she said in her desperation. 'She would tell Mr Jarrett everything.'

It was more of a bark than a laugh.

'You forget that Henry Jarrett and I are friends,' he said. 'We are members of the same society. Do you really think he would turn his back on a brother just for you?'

She was thinking hard and fast, but nothing was coming that could get her out of a mess that was not of her making.

'You might still report me,' she whispered hoarsely.

'There would be nothing to stop you.'

'But why should I? If my gentlemen like what they see I'll have to be more imaginative next time. Right now it's just a matter of letting them see what you are made of.' Trimmer waited for a response but nothing came. The fight, if it could be called that, was out of her. When he placed a hand on her chest she made no attempt to remove it, but let her arms hang loosely by her side, even when he unbuttoned a few buttons at her throat and drew her vest far enough out to see her breasts. Then he laid his hands on her shoulders and pressed her downwards until she dropped to her knees and stared dumbly as his fingers flicked open his buttons. When they were free he started on the small mother-of-pearl ones on his white cotton johns. 'I think you'll do well. In fact, you'd better.'

When Henry Jarrett and Charlie Grant returned from Chadwick Avenue, Tommy Quinn was in the process of hanging a large map in the middle of the wall facing the largest window.

'This is a 2,500 to 1, sir. Approximately two feet to the mile.' Tommy Quinn was looking decidedly pleased with himself. 'I had to sign for it, sir.'

'Then don't tear it,' Inspector Grant offered, 'or you'll be living on bugger all.'

'Ignore the Highlander,' Jarrett said, peering closely at the map. 'You've done very well, Sergeant.'

'Thank you, sir.' Quinn looked concerned, as though almost frightened to ask. 'Mrs MacNiven, sir?'

'Right as rain. She received a visit from someone who identified himself as the mysterious Mr Lorimer. A few minutes later she discovered him in the act of searching beneath the floorboards in Fenton's room. When he rushed at her, probably because he thought she was going to scream, she passed out but luckily didn't injure herself. The boy who ran to alert us was a neighbour's lad.'

Sergeant Quinn gave this a little thought.

'That account doesn't paint Lorimer as a murderer, sir,' he said after a few moments.

'That's what Inspector Grant was saying in the wagon. Why would a man who had knifed his partners to death so expertly leave someone alive who could identify him?'

'He wouldn't, so the killer is another party entirely and Lorimer is the one who is in danger.'

'It is beginning to look that way,' Jarrett agreed. 'But how do we know there are three Canadians in the gang and not thirty-three?'

'Lorimer is a Canadian, sir?'

'He told Mrs MacNiven he was Thaddeus Lorimer, Fenton's cousin, although I think we can throw that relationship out of the window. He was merely trying to gain entry to the house because he was looking for something.'

'Do we know what, sir?'

'Inspector Grant and I were speculating that he may have been looking for the telescope and cane, but that is as wild a guess as any other. Truth is, we have no idea. The space beneath the floor was devoid of anything larger than a mouse dropping, but whether that means he found what he was looking for or not is anybody's guess.' Jarrett fell silent for a few moments, while he studied the area around Chadwick Avenue. 'One thing we can say is that Lorimer, Fenton and Hartman were members of the same gang. Lorimer knew where both of the others were lodging. That could, of course, mean he was either a friend or an enemy, but the letter Hartman sent to Fenton stated that 'T.L. had called upon him despite his firm instructions', I think the phrase was. This more or less proves that they were all the one bunch.'

'And that Hartman was in a position to order the others around.'

'Yes, that too.' While he was talking, Superintendent Jarrett was inserting a fresh stick of blue chalk into the gripper of his large wooden compass. He then expanded the wooden arms to eighteen inches and tightened the brass wing nut. 'I hope this wipes off.'

'Not as much as I do, sir,' Sergeant Quinn admitted.

The yard-wide circle completed to his own satisfaction, Henry Jarrett stood back and considered his handiwork.

'Takes in a fair bit,' he observed.

'Just about everything,' said Charlie Grant, his feet already throbbing and he hadn't even left the office. 'Can we cut it down to the high points?'

'Fine.' Jarrett used the cane as a pointer and caused young Quinn to grimace each time he jabbed the linen map. 'Yorkhill, Dowanhill, Kelvingrove . . . '

'Yorkhill is a private estate,' Grant said. 'I doubt if he would have been allowed to swan around there every day.'

'And Dowanhill is the observatory,' Tommy Quinn offered. 'I think they've already got a telescope.'

Jarrett smiled at the preposterousness of that.

'First, you don't look at the sky by day, and second, this is a terrestrial telescope. That, gentlemen, is the sum total of my knowledge.'

'Maybe we shouldn't dismiss Dowanhill so

easily,' said Charlie Grant. 'There are good views all round.'

'Anything that might be of special interest to criminals?'

'Hyndland Station? Royal Botanic Gardens?'

Jarrett was less than impressed.

'There is nothing else for it,' he said. 'We are going to have to do the walk. You take Dowanhill, Inspector, and young Quinn here can scout the high ground in Kelvingrove. I will pay a visit to Yorkhill House and see if my betters have anything to say.'

* * *

Thaddeus Lorimer tugged open the securing bow on the bundle he had retrieved from Fenton's lodgings, cautiously turned back the canvas flaps and even more tentatively lifted the Adams. Fenton was the trigger-man, not him, but Fenton and Hartman were dead now and that left him with no choice but to see it through. Problem was, the Ghost knew them, where they were and everywhere they went. He knew nothing.

Seeing the others laid out like that in the waiting-room of the city mortuary brought it all home to him with a vengeance. The one who had slain them so efficiently must have tracked him too, and he found that thought terrifying. He may have been within yards of him the day he visited Hartman, and he might even have followed him when he called on Mrs MacNiven. He could be anyone, anywhere, and he could strike at any time.

Lorimer had never been comfortable with guns. He was a planner and thinker, and it had annoyed him mightily when Hartman was appointed leader of the group. As far as Lorimer could make out, Hartman's primary skill lay in bullying people and making them stay in line. He had certainly been abusive to him when boredom and concern over lack of progress had driven him to the Sweeney house. But that was all in the past now. He, Lorimer, was sorry when he heard about Fenton. Hartman, on the other hand, got what was coming to him. Unfortunately, the faceless one — known as the Ghost by the Pinkerton men — cared nothing for a man's qualities. He had his shopping list.

Fenton, who knew about these things, explained the benefits of the English Adams to his tyro cohorts, just in case something happened to him and they had to defend themselves. It was a .44 double action weapon, which meant that pulling the trigger rotated the cylinder, cocked the hammer and then released it to do its work, all in one go.

Not having to cock the hammer with the thumb might just buy that extra second or so, Fenton had said. It was also of the solid frame type, in that the barrel and stock were of one piece and was considered to be superior to the Colt revolvers, which had hinged frames. At the time Lorimer had not really been paying attention because nothing was going to happen to Fenton. He was just exaggerating.

Lorimer rose from his chair and stood by the narrow window, watching for some sign of danger. He remained for several minutes within the shadow of the curtain in case any one of those small tenement windows on the other side of the street harboured the Ghost. Hartman and Fenton may have been stabbed to death, but that didn't preclude some other means in his case. This time it might be a sniper's rifle with a sighting tube. In the right hands such a device could be very deadly indeed.

How strange it was, he thought, the way things had been turned around. They had been told to seek out, identify and destroy him. Now he was destroying them, one by one . . .

7

Inspector Charlie Grant reached the iron gates of the observatory after a long, foot-burning climb up from the road that had been named after this scientific establishment. Everything had a certain newness about it, which street names like Observatory Road, Victoria Circus, Victoria Crescent and the rest attested to. Its presence here was, of course, a matter of necessity. The old observatory in High Street had served the purpose admirably until industry had taken precedence over curiosity and tall chimneys had sprouted up all round. By the time Professor Nichol obtained a Treasury grant to build this beautiful replacement on what was known as Horselethill, fog and smog had taken the place of air in the city centre.

Grant pushed open the smallest of the two gates and was immediately joined by a stiff-backed, middle-aged sort with all the bearing of an old soldier.

'Sir!' he said loudly. It was like a punch on the nose. 'How may I help you?'

The brass badge was held up in front of his

eyes so that he didn't have to bend his stiff neck.

'Detective Inspector Grant. Who's in charge?'

'Nobody at all right now, sir. Doctor Ainsley and the others will be along from the university later, but at the moment it is you and me.'

'Then you'll have to do.' Charlie produced his half-plate prints. 'Either of these characters familiar to you?'

The old soldier looked and frowned and shook his head.

'Sorry, sir,' he said. 'Never laid eyes on them.'

'They're quite dead, of course.'

'That's obvious, sir. It's the life-spark, you know.'

'Meaning?'

'I used to see that during the Indian Mutiny. Once the life-spark is gone it's not the same person.'

Without quite knowing why, Charlie Grant got the feeling that the man was being deliberately evasive.

'Presumably you are empowered to show me around,' he said, returning the pictures to his inside pocket. 'I could always insist.'

The man nodded, then turned abruptly and led the way up the driveway to the side entrance. The building itself was all on one level, save for the high dome to the rear.

Charlie Grant had no real idea of what went on in an observatory, other than a half-formed image of crazed scientists running around with telescopes and butterfly nets in search of moon-men. But this was nothing more than a collection of rooms and desks, like a school without pupils. After a few minutes he returned to the good fresh air and the encircling path.

'We will take a tour around the building,' he said. 'You can tell me everything you can see out there.'

'Me, sir?'

'You, sir. I want to see the surrounding district through your eyes. I want to know what you think is important.'

'As you wish, sir, but I really have no idea what you are hoping to find.' The ramrod-straight gatehouse-keeper commenced his encirclement of the building by indicating westward. 'Jordanhill Railway Station and to the north-west is the Royal Lunatic Asylum. Due north is Kelvinside Academy.' A little further on he said, 'Royal Botanic Gardens to the west and Infirmary to the south-west.' When he reached the front of the observatory and was level with the gates he concluded with, 'Southward is the River Clyde where it is joined by the River Kelvin. You can see the cotton factory, the Tod & MacGregor Shipbuilding Yard where they make steam-boats and Fairfield's Engineering works. That's about it, sir, apart from perhaps several thousand things in between.'

'Well,' Charlie said, 'you have been most helpful. I thank you, Sergeant.'

The stiff man looked down his long nose at him.

'How did you know I was a sergeant, sir,' he asked.

'Just a wild guess.' Before pulling open the gate and taking his leave, Inspector Grant asked, 'Could anyone come up here and survey the city if they felt like it?'

'No reason why not, sir. Strictly speaking you are supposed to get permission from the university, but most don't bother. And anyway, this astronomy lark is quite fashion-able at the moment. The toffs come and go as they please in their fancy carriages, so why shouldn't the other ladies and gents enjoy the facilities.'

* * *

Yorkhill House was the home of Mrs Jane Gordon, whose family had amassed its fortune in the West Indies. It was a substantial mansion with a staff of twenty-two persons, including the gardeners and stable-hands. There was sufficient grassland all around to race a horse or discharge a rifle without fear of doing ill to anyone. But progress was no longer confined to the horizon. Sooner or later it would reach the very gates.

When the house was built, a mere sixty or so years earlier, the merchant Robert Fulton Alexander could consider all the lands around to be his personal playground. The vale of the River Kelvin and Pear-Tree Well were thickly wooded glens and such other habitations as existed were the homes of craftsmen who followed their trades quietly and with dignity. The only nod in the direction of industry, if it could be called that, was in the cluster of picturesque mills by the Kelvin river. They had been given in perpetuity by the Regent Murray to the baxters — or bakers — of the district as a reward for feeding his army and assisting in the defeat of his half-sister, Mary, Queen of Scots. Now the ground between the house and the mills was cut clean across by improvements to Old Dumbarton Road and Ferry Road. To the south the curse of the railway was marked by the black scar of the Stobcross branch line, although that alone could not be accused of marring the view of the Clyde. The building of steamboats involved iron and that meant furnaces and chimneys, smoke and filth. But worst of all it meant people and people lived in tenements.

Jane Gordon was neither young nor old and if really unlucky would live to see the full industrialization of the area. Even though her world was under threat she still knew exactly how to nail Henry Jarrett's hide to the wall.

'I am surprised that the chief constable did not tell me of your interest in Yorkhill House,' she said. They were in a drawing-room that was larger than most houses and decorated with the treasures of the Orient. Although the family's wealth had come from the Caribbean there was little here to suggest that. 'Mr and Mrs Rattray were my guests only last Saturday. We have been friends for a very long time.'

Superintendent Jarrett had the overwhelming feeling of having strolled naively into a scorpion's nest and would have to keep his nerve if he wished to get out unharmed, professionally speaking. It was almost certain that before he made it back to headquarters one of Mrs Gordon's men would have reached Rattray with a letter complaining about the ranks no longer knowing their place. It was essential, therefore, that he, Jarrett, could give a damned good account of himself. Not that Rattray would be in the mood to listen. He never was.

Since confusing the enemy was the best form of defence, Jarrett turned his attention to the wall-hanging on the right of the large Adam fireplace. By rights this clash of cultures ought to have jarred dreadfully, but somehow it worked and they had learned to live harmoniously.

'*Ni Tsan*,' he said quietly. 'Trees after rain captured perfectly in a few ink strokes.'

Mrs Gordon kept her own council for a few moments, then said, 'You know China, Superintendent.'

'I was twenty years in the Orient. I joined the Hong Kong police after the Treaty.'

'How very interesting,' she said, then, 'You have expressed an interest in talking to my staff. May I ask why?'

'I am trying to put a name to a face,' Jarrett replied, although that was not entirely true. 'I merely thought that one of the servants might recognize him.'

'But why here in particular?'

'For reasons I can't go into my men and I are checking all the high ground in the district.'

'For?'

'This individual may have been observing something out there in the city and we would like to know what.'

Mrs Gordon looked mildly concerned.

'By your tone I assume this person is a criminal,' she said. 'You are not telling me that you brought him with you in that wagon thing out there.'

'No, madam, I have a photograph of him.'

'Then show it to me.'

Jarrett produced the picture of Fenton, but did not initially place it into her outstretched hand.

'I'm afraid he is dead, Mrs Gordon,' he warned.

'Good.' She took the print and nodded approvingly. For a moment or two Jarrett thought he had brought home the bacon. Then she said, 'I have never seen him before.'

'Perhaps the staff . . . '

'I shouldn't think so. I do not permit them to consort with strangers.'

Jarrett knew that whatever he said would be wrong, because people like Mrs Gordon did not take kindly to an assumption of equality by a mere police superintendent. What they wanted was deference, so that when she expressed the opinion that her servants could not identify the deceased she expected the matter to end there and then. But it didn't.

'With all due respect, madam,' Jarrett said, 'I'm afraid I must insist.'

Jane Gordon was less than pleased but had been raised never to reveal her inner feelings. She would comply, but there would be a price to pay. The small brass bell brought the butler immediately.

'Superintendent Jarrett has the run of the house, Mason,' she said. 'Escort him to wherever he wishes to commence, then come back here for your instructions.'

Henry Jarrett took his leave of her and followed Mason down to the large pantry where the footmen would be cleaning the silver and, until Mason arrived, exchanging the news of the day. It was as good, or as bad, a place to start as any.

* * *

Kelvingrove Park was new. It was the first specially created park in Scotland and was designed by Sir Joseph Paxton, whose finest work was London's Crystal Palace. It was also unashamedly intended for use by the middle classes, who felt uncomfortable promenading in the more working-class Glasgow Green.

The three-tier granite staircase, built of polished ashlar slabs, seemed to reach into the clouds. By the time Sergeant Quinn finally got to the double gateway on the upper terrace he was ready for a seat. But was it the same seat Fenton used to survey the city, or that part of it which concerned him? At first it was just a disappointing and disparate jumble of warehouses and factories, with no beginning, no end and no order, but little by little he started to identify individual places, starting with Gilmorehill, the Infirmary and, a little to the left, Yorkhill House, where Superintendent Jarrett may or may not be finding success.

Tommy Quinn continued to think of Hartman and his cohorts as a criminal gang because nothing else made sense. Decent, law-abiding men did not send each other cryptic letters, or skulk around with telescopes. And they certainly didn't wind up in alleyways in ungodly hours with peculiar knife wounds on their bodies and not a coin or match to their name. The fact that Mrs MacNiven spoke highly of Fenton and Lorimer displayed a marked reluctance to be violent did not alter anything. They were villains doing what villains do best — plot, connive and steal.

But steal what and from whom? And while he was speculating, was Lorimer alive or dead? Had this gang now been completely wiped out by a rival outfit? If so, there was absolutely no way of knowing who they were or what they were planning to do. Normally something of a guarded optimist, Tommy Quinn suddenly felt such an overwhelming sense of hopelessness that it drove his spirits down into his size tens.

At Tod & MacGregor's shipyard on the north bank of the Clyde, and visible from Kelvingrove, Yorkhill and Dowanhill, the first of three identical hulls slid down a ramp and bobbed aimlessly in the river, where tiny, faceless men commenced securing her with tow-lines in preparation for being dragged to the fitting out basin.

* * *

Jimmy Lyle had been waiting patiently in the grove to the east of the big house for Jarrett to clamber into the Kinross wagon and leave. This time he hoped there would be something to show for it. It had cost him good money to tail the police vehicle in a public cab and his editor, Jake McGovern, was getting impatient for what he, Lyle, had assured him was something big. Certainly, he had been first with the innocent man story and for that reason alone he was free to follow his nose. But only up to a point.

During the ninety minutes or so that the detective had been there, the police driver had twice left the vehicle in the care of the single, highly trained horse, the first time for a cup of tea and anything else that was going in the kitchen, and second to visit the privy. On both occasions he had passed within twenty feet of the newsman without glancing right or left.

Lyle gave the wagon a good three or four minutes to get down the drive to the large gates before leaving the protection of the ash wood and hurrying over to the kitchen door. Just as he got there a scullery maid emerged with a bucket of vegetable tops for the midden. She was only prevented from screaming by a hand over her mouth and a bright shilling in front of her eyes.

'That policeman who just left,' Lyle said softly, 'did you talk to him?'

'No, he didn't think the maids and kitchen staff would have any information. He's right enough, because we're always in here and never see anyone.'

'Who, then?'

'The butler and the rest of them up there.' The girl raised an eyebrow when it was obvious that he was unsure of what she meant, then added, 'The housekeeper and footmen, and the stable and garden staff. It was only the ones who might have seen somebody.'

'Do you know who he was looking for?'

The girl shook her head and made it clear that she shouldn't be lingering this way.

'I've got to go,' she whispered hoarsely. 'I'll get an earful from the cook. Or worse. It's instant dismissal if you're caught talking to men inside or outside the house.'

Then she was gone and Jimmy Lyle was faced with deciding who to approach next. But at least the girl had narrowed the field and for that he was grateful.

From what little he knew about the working of the mansions, the types she had mentioned within the house were the ones who had most to lose and were therefore least likely to be forthcoming. The butler was the worst of all when it came to protecting his betters and bolstering their position in the world. He it was who took the orders of the day from them and passed them on to the pyramid of servants. And it was he who informed his superiors of the need to praise or punish. He brought the mail, and served as barber and shaver to the master of the house. He served the meals, along with the footmen, supervised the polishing of the silver in the pantry and, at the end of what was usually a long and hectic day, made sure that all lights were out and that all doors and windows were firmly secured. This man, for one, would be unlikely to betray confidences for a couple of sovs.

Having guessed correctly that he stood little chance of remaining undetected and at large in there for very long, Lyle kept under window level until he had reached the rear of the property and the large cobblestoned yard around which stood the stables and the coaching sheds. The latter were closed and barred, but almost certainly housed a landau and brougham, whatever else. There was no sign of a coachman, and just the right amount of activity among the unsupervised grooms and stable hands that one might expect.

Lyle chose one stable boy and made straight for him, while the others suddenly found something to do and set about doing it. The reporter was wearing a suit, after all, and that was quite good enough for them. Staff at that level never questioned a suit, or looked at its face. They just vanished.

The boy who had been propping up the slatted wooden wall realized that whatever he did would be wrong. It was too late by far to scurry to the right or left and pretend to be busy, particularly as he had nothing to be busy with.

Then his luck did a complete about turn

and he stared at the handful of shillings in the stranger's palm.

'Some information, son,' Jimmy Lyle said. 'Let's say a couple of bob's worth for starters.'

The boy jerked his head to indicate an open door and empty stable.

'Out of the light,' he said quickly. 'They've got eyes everywhere, those buggers.'

Inside the darkened building Lyle said 'The policeman, Jarrett, must have talked to the outside staff. What was he after?'

The boy shrugged.

'He wanted to know if we'd seen a gent with a telescope around here.'

Jimmy Lyle gave a sharp laugh.

'Telescope? Are you sure?'

'That's what he said. The house would have had to know about it, of course. He couldn't wander around here without their permission.'

Lyle gave this some thought.

'What about this character?' he asked after a few moments. Somehow and in some way it had to do with the latest killing, but Jarrett and company were keeping everything close to their proverbial waistcoats and giving out nothing at all. Not even Sergeant Davie Black on the desk was able to furnish him with much. It was as though the Detective

Department suspected a leak within their own ranks and were being doubly guarded. 'Did he say what he was doing with the telescope and why it was important enough for the police to take an interest?'

'He didn't say anything, just asked questions.'

'There must be something happening.' Since it was plain that the stable boy was becoming fearful of surprise at any moment, Lyle said, 'Look, I'll make it five shillings if you can give me anything I can use.'

The boy looked past him at the bright yard out there. One of these moments someone was going to catch him out. But at the same time five bob was more than he earned in a week. That was a terrible temptation.

'I don't know anything about the police or the odd gent,' he said hurriedly, 'but I can tell you about some funny goings-on.'

'Try me.'

'Well, I only came here about three months ago. Right away I was warned to keep my mouth shut because I would probably hear and see things that were none of my business.' The boy was churning inside. His desire for the five shillings was at war with his fear of saying too much. 'Ever heard of Darnwood Mansion.'

'Couldn't honestly swear to it.'

'Then find out where it is and I'll bet you thank me for it.'

Lyle shook his head.

'Come on, son,' he said. 'You're going to have to do better than that for your five bob.'

'Right.' The boy was getting desperate now because there was only so long you could push your luck. 'I was up front with the coachman one evening when we took the lady to Darnwood Mansion. I never saw so many carriages. We were all told to return home and come back later for our masters and mistresses because they didn't know what to do with all the staff. Truth is, they didn't want us nosing about and trying to find out what was going on.'

'But you did.'

'Too bloody sure I did. One of the girls up there told me it was one of those so-called drinking parties where they all wear masks. Get me? Masks and bugger all else.' The boy moved to the door and looked all ways to see if the coast was clear. Then he gestured for his five shillings. 'No guarantees, or anything, but we've been put on late duty for the evening after next. It's up to you what you want to do with that.'

Then he was gone, leaving Jimmy Lyle to somehow make his way back down to the Old Dumbarton Road without getting spotted.

* * *

The dozen or so chalk crosses, rough circles and question-marks Superintendent Jarrett had made did not in any way improve Sergeant Quinn's mood. On top of what he felt was a most unproductive trip to the park, there was now the distinct possibility of having to pay for the borrowed map.

'To be perfectly honest, sir,' he said, 'it was everything and nothing. Any factory or store might be a target. But when you are up there you realize how hopeless it all is.'

'Too true.' Charlie Grant added. 'You probably got more than we did, Superintendent. At least you found out about the Bacchanalian knees-up.'

Walking into the butler's pantry and finding Ronald Farley, the second footman, polishing the silver had been probably the only lucky break of the day. There had been no need to introduce himself. The look on Farley's face said it all. It was the pleading expression of a man trying hard to go straight, a man whose entire future lay in the palm of Jarrett's hand.

Luckily for Farley, Henry Jarrett was not a vindictive man. After all, a reformed character was one less villain on the street, even if the references that got him into the big house were probably as bona fide as a lead florin.

So it was from Farley that the superintendent learned first about the masque at Darnwood Mansion, and then about the guest list, or as much of it as he could piece together from the staff of the two properties. But if Jarrett was not spiteful, he was at least protective of his garnered information. He did not share everything with the others in the Detective Department. There were names on the list that were well worth keeping up his mandarin's sleeve for the proverbial rainy day.

'It may be immoral, Inspector,' he said, 'but it isn't illegal.'

'It might be if it is used to entrap.'

'You mean blackmail?'

'That's the obvious risk in getting involved with that sort of nonsense.' Grant paused, then added, 'So if you are looking for someone to go in undercover, I don't mind volunteering.'

'I don't doubt it for a minute,' Jarrett replied. 'But don't worry, Inspector, I wouldn't put you to such an embarrassment. I already have someone reporting back to me.'

Charlie Grant feigned disappointment while young Quinn tried hard not to laugh. After a few moments the Inspector said, 'Do you mind if I say something about the elusive weapon?'

'Please do,' Jarrett said. 'I'll accept anything.'

'I was thinking about a knife-thrower.'

There was silence for a few moments, then:

'Go on.'

'Well, to be honest I don't know much about the art, but it might be worth considering.' Grant let this sink in. 'I once arrested a thrower in the Trongate. He claimed to be able to toss a pack of cards into the air, then throw a knife into them and pin one of the aces to a board. But after a while I got it into my head that he was a fraudster, so I pinched him. What he was doing was pushing a knife into an ace, which he concealed in his hand when holding the blade. Then he would toss the rest of the pack into the air and throw the knife at the board. It was all done very quickly, so no one could see the card on the blade. Big cheers and plenty of pennies until I spoiled it and marched him off. If I remember right he was fined five bob and advised to move on.'

'Perhaps that's what drove him mad,' Tommy Quinn said. 'Now he is killing people in the hope of getting his five shillings back.'

Jarrett laughed, but soon raised a hand to restore order.

'Are you seriously suggesting that we may be looking for a knife-thrower, Inspector Grant?' he asked.

'As things stand, I would quite happily consider anything. And it is the Glasgow Fair, after all. If you can't find one of them on the Green right now you never will.'

'Good point.' The superintendent mulled this over. 'Motive?'

'None needed. Whoever it is that wanted Hartman and Fenton out of the way finds a knife-artist and makes it well worth his while.'

'I'll go along with the throwing idea,' Jarrett said, 'but I'm not sure it would be that easy to get someone who would be willing to murder for money. Still, if you are willing to tour the side-shows, you may proceed. But don't take too long over it. It's only a theory, after all.'

They agreed that it was too late now to pursue that particular line, since many of the stall-holders would have packed up for the day and those who hadn't were probably too drunk or fed-up to answer questions. Better start again in the morning, Inspector Grant agreed. He was easily talked into it.

Anyway, Superintendent Jarrett felt that he had kept Rattray waiting for just as long as was prudent. The CC had left a message at the desk saying he wanted to talk to Jarrett when he got back from Yorkhill House. Jarrett had sent a note back upstairs by a nervous young constable who could use a bit of experience, saying that he was briefing his men and was on the verge of a major break-through in the knife killings. Never was anything further from the truth, but it was exactly what the chief constable wanted to hear and Jarrett hoped it might just make the confrontation a shade less unpleasant.

* * *

Chief Constable Rattray was rarely over-worked, yet could always manage to give the impression of being up to the ears in it. Essential to this illusion was his seeming inability to remain seated for more than a few seconds at a time.

'Right, Jarrett,' he said, yet his expression lacked the hardness the superintendent had come to expect. 'I gather you saw fit to make yourself disagreeable to Mrs Gordon of Yorkhill House.'

'I wasn't conscious of that, sir.' Henry Jarrett watched Rattray's travels between the filing drawers and the bright window as he performed some obscure ritual with a sheaf of ancient papers. It was all nonsense, of course. Same papers, same perambulations. Nothing ever changed. 'I was following up a possible line of enquiry and found Mrs Gordon perfectly amenable. I apologize if I offended the lady.'

Rattray stared at him for a few moments, then quite uncharacteristically gestured for him to sit while he made himself comfortable in a large padded chair which was more inducive to dozing than working.

'Perhaps I misunderstood her,' he said. 'It was a brief note and I took from it that she considered herself to be under suspicion.'

'With respect, sir,' Jarrett replied, 'nothing could be further from the truth. My visit to Yorkhill House was part of a wider investigation into the elevated points in the district. You will recall the memo I sent you concerning the second victim, Fenton, and his penchant for peering through telescopes.'

Rattray blinked at the various sheets of yellow paper that covered much of his desk.

'Absolutely,' he said, nodding. 'And you were looking . . . '

'For a possible vantage point he may have used.'

'Of course you were.' The CC continued to stare at Jarrett and gave every indication of being interested in Herbert Fenton. 'Did you find it?'

'We think we may have done, sir, but it is

early days yet and I would prefer not to commit myself.'

'Very wise, very wise.' Now that he had disposed of such a triviality as murder, Chief Constable Rattray leaned forward, clasped his hands and said, 'Mrs Gordon's household staff, Jarrett.'

'Sir?'

'Were they helpful? What I am trying to say is were they forthcoming? Did you find them a useful source of information about . . . well, anything?'

'I'm afraid not, sir,' the superintendent lied. 'But that is no more than I would expect from a well-run house. Mrs Gordon can compliment herself on the loyalty and discretion of every member of her staff.'

Rattray raised one eyebrow, then both as he tried to read Jarrett's mind and failed utterly.

'The lady will be delighted to hear that,' he said, rising slowly and resting on clenched knuckles. 'May I also let her know that your enquiries vis-à-vis Yorkhill House have been satisfactorily concluded?'

'Indeed you may, sir.' Jarrett got to his feet and felt suddenly pleased at the smooth way the meeting had gone. Knowledge is power, they say, but suspicion of knowledge can be just as powerful. 'Unless we can place Fenton at the house at any time, because that could only have happened with Mrs Gordon's knowledge and approval.'

As he took his leave, Jarrett felt glad that Rattray could not number knife-throwing among his few skills.

* * *

Since the encounter with the chief constable had been considerably more amicable than he had any reason to expect, Henry Jarrett treated himself to a nice example of a Bracken Fern from the Gardener's Emporium and escorted it home to Mrs Maitland's superior guest house for respectable single gentlemen. There he let it look out of the window for a few minutes while he opened the Wardian case and held a discussion with himself as to exactly where it should go. He also wiped the moisture from the glass and added a little fresh water to the pool to compensate. The Bracken Fern, he eventually decided, should overhang the little fisherman and protect him from the sun, such as there was.

He was replacing the glazed lid when there was a gentle rapping at the door and Mrs Maitland entered soundlessly and closed the door behind her in exactly the same way. As ever, she declined to sit but chose instead to close in on him by the indoor glasshouse and communicate by whispers.

'I am a little bit concerned about Lizzie,' she said softly. 'The girl is normally quite cheerful and chatty, but she has become sullen and uncommunicative.'

Henry Jarrett, who knew as much about women's problems as the little pottery figure, thought this over briefly.

'A young man?' he suggested. It was the obvious thing to say and covered everything from a broken heart to an unfortunate state of affairs.

'No,' Elsie Maitland replied swiftly, shaking her head. 'She only gets one half-day off a fortnight and she spends that with her mother in Carmyle.'

After wondering for a few moments why Mrs Maitland had even bothered mentioning it, Jarrett asked, 'Do you want me to talk to her?'

'Oh, I don't think so. You would only scare her.'

'That is the last thing I would wish,' the superintendent said and meant it. 'You tell her from me that I would be only too happy to listen to her if there is any way I can be of help.'

'Yes, Henry,' Elsie Maitland said, 'I know you would, and I am sure her mind will be greatly eased by knowing that you have her interests at heart.'

8

According to the large board at the entrance to Glasgow Green, they were all there: fat women, thin women, bearded women, fire-eaters, jugglers, a variety of peep-shows, two waxworks, a circus, several shooting galleries, fortune tellers and traders from every part of Britain. On all sides, near and far, brightly coloured theatres of wood and canvas stood out higher and larger than neighbouring stalls, while troupes of three or four actors vied with their competitors at the top of their voices. Colour and noise attracted the curious; familiar and unfamiliar smells attracted the hungry.

Charlie Grant weaved his way in and out of the throng as he searched for knife-throwers. Had he been looking for artists or palmists knives would have been thudding to the right and left of him, but as it was there was a dearth of spinning blades and not a rotating wheel to be seen.

Just as he reached a gin stall a young woman suddenly materialized in front of him, realized who and what he was, and quickly turned away. But she wasn't quick enough.

Grant's fingers bit into her shoulder and spun her around.

'Don't worry, Maisie,' he said. 'I'm looking for bigger fish.'

That appeared to relax her and she even came close to smiling.

'Information costs.'

'You know I can't be seen giving money to your sort. If you can help out I'll leave a few bob with the desk sergeant for you.'

'Not bloody likely.' Again, she made an attempt to escape, but as before was prevented from doing so. 'What is it, anyway?'

'I'm looking for a knife-thrower.'

'Why? What's he done?'

'Probably nothing. All I want is advice.'

She laughed then and for a moment lost her hardness and became almost doll-like. Her rosy cheeks and painted lips added to the effect, but otherwise condemned her. Good women, as they styled themselves, sought the porcelain look and achieved it by staying out of the sun, powdering their faces with talcum powder or white flour, and drinking plenty of vinegar water. Only Maisie's kind used cosmetics.

'Decided to kill that Superintendent Jarrett?' she giggled. 'Not before bloody time.'

'No, nothing as drastic as that.' Charlie released her now that she had quit trying to flee. 'Now, tell me and save my shoe leather. Where are the knife-throwers?'

'There is only one,' she replied, 'or there was.'

'What do you mean?'

'He up and fled early yesterday morning. When all the stall-holders arrived to set up for the day his pitch was empty. Not that he had much to take, of course. He wasn't one of them who used the big wheel, or anything like that. Didn't have an assistant. Too mean probably. All he had was his board and a few knives.'

'What was his routine?'

'He'd invite people up from the crowd and either take an apple clean off their heads, or chop their cigar in two. They did it to show off, the stupid buggers. He was the one who kept the collection.'

'What was his name?'

'Amen-Seth, descendant from Phobos, king of the Nile, or some such shit.'

'His real name.'

'Harold something.'

'Any idea where he was really from?'

Maisie shrugged expansively.

'London, I think. He was here last year and did the whole fortnight, but this time he upped sticks after a couple of days. It must have been some time during the night, because he was gone and his pitch was empty three mornings ago. Don't ask me where he went, because I don't know.'

Grant dug out a half-crown and slid it across the wooden trestle to the gin-seller.

'Give Maisie a double and the change,' he said with a wink, then turned again to the young woman. She disposed of the cup in short time and happily collected her assortment of coins. 'One last question, does he have a cart?'

She nodded.

'One of those butcher's van things and an old nag. Once it's all closed up the van's like a wee house. Quite snug and private, and he doesn't have to pay rent.'

'How do you know?'

'How do you think I know? There's more to life than chucking knives.'

⋆ ⋆ ⋆

When Charlie Grant returned to Central and related the limited information he had garnered, Superintendent Jarrett was obliged to agree that the knife-thrower's disappearance at that particular time seemed to be more than coincidental. Although there was not one shred of evidence to link the man with the murders of Hartman and Fenton, it was decided that he ought to be located and brought back for questioning. Sergeant Quinn, therefore, was given the task of contacting all major police offices within a reasonable distance in the hope that the man had erected his stall, such as it was, where he might reasonably be spotted.

It was in the early afternoon that a wire was received from the City of Edinburgh Police to confirm that Amen-Seth had been apprehended in the Grassmarket, where he had set up his pitch and was attracting a considerable crowd. He was now in custody and awaiting instructions from Glasgow. Since it was Inspector Grant's idea he took himself off to Queen's Street Railway Station and caught a train for Edinburgh Haymarket, where he would receive the suspect and escort him back to Glasgow along with the tools of his trade. His horse and van were to be stabled in the police barracks on the off-chance that he would again obtain his freedom and not give his farewell performance on the gallows at Jail Square.

The return journey took four hours, so it was a little after six o'clock when a Black Maria, drawn by two dray horses, arrived at the entrance to the Central and the inspector, with a very unlikely Egyptian in tow, proceeded along the oak-panelled main corridor to the offices of the Detective Department.

He was in his middle years and wiry. His moustache, and there was plenty of it, would not have disgraced a senior army man. Henry Jarrett, who had expected a shifty-eyed rogue was pleasantly disappointed.

'John Harold Rumsen,' the man answered in reply to Jarrett's first question. The canvas roll with its double-wound and neatly bowed blue ribbon lay in the middle of the desk. 'Stepney Green in the County of Middlesex, but not for these many years.'

The superintendent drew open the faded ribbon and spread the roll. There were six knives, all identical. Jarrett lifted one of them and examined it for a few moments. The blade was an elongated leaf shape. The handle was as plain as plain could be.

'Is this a typical throwing knife?' he asked casually.

'They come in many shapes, sir. What matters is the balance. The centre of gravity should be halfway along its length.'

The superintendent placed the knife on an extended index finger and nodded admiringly.

'Why did you depart so suddenly, Mr Rumsen?'

The showman hadn't quite expected such a

change of tack and was momentarily stuck for words.

'To be frank,' he said at length, 'I owe a certain character money since last year and he was coming round to collect in the morning. I thought it best not to be there.'

'Sounds plausible,' Jarrett said. 'Now why don't you tell me the truth?'

'That is the truth.'

'No, Mr Rumsen, it isn't. If you owed a small amount you could probably earn that in a day or two. If it was a large amount you would have avoided the Green like the plague. Either way your story rings like a wooden bell.'

Rumsen stared at his toecaps for some time, then sighed long and said, 'I was approached and put in a bad position.'

'Approached by whom?'

'I don't know his name or anything about him. All I know is that he scared the hell out of me. He had a cold way about him, so there was no need for threats.'

'What did he want?'

'What do you think, Superintendent? It wasn't a birthday cake.'

'He wanted you to kill a man,' Jarrett said. It was not a question.

'Yes.'

'Who?'

'Again, I have no idea. Not that it mattered, because I wasn't interested.'

'Did you tell him that?'

'No. I didn't have the guts. He is one of those people who don't take excuses, if you know what I mean. So I told him I would have to think about it. All I wanted to do was clear off before he came back for his answer.'

'What exactly was it you were afraid of?'

'Him, of course. The way I saw it, once he had made me an offer that was that. If I said no he couldn't very well leave me alive, not after seeing his face. I would have been a bloody menace to him as long as I was upright and breathing.'

Jarrett briefly glanced at Grant and Quinn in turn and got a curt nod from each. Rumsen was telling the truth.

'Tell me,' the Superintendent said, 'did he have an accent? Was he, for example, a Canadian?'

'No, nothing like that. One of your home-grown blokes, I'd say, or not a kick and a spit away from your fair city, no pun intended.'

'How much did he offer you, Mr Rumsen?' Jarrett continued.

'Two hundred.'

'That's a considerable amount of money. Weren't you tempted?'

'Not to kill someone, no. But if he had paid me in advance I would have gone a damned sight further than Edinburgh.'

Jarrett laid the knife down and smiled pleasantly at the fairground entertainer.

'He might have been joking, of course, or just crazy. We get plenty of them in here.'

'You may take it from me, sir, the man was in deadly earnest.'

'That being the case, perhaps you could furnish us with a description of this individual. Whether or not he has anything to do with the case in hand, we certainly can't have him hunting the city in search of someone who is prepared to carry out a murder for him.'

Rumsen gave the matter some thought, then said, 'He was of medium height and clean-shaven, and his clothes seemed not to fit him too well, as though he had recently been ill and lost weight. But the most striking features were his eyes. They were very light blue, so that sometimes when he turned his head he appeared almost to be blind. He wasn't, of course, which is was what made him so scary. That and his flat voice. There was no feeling, no humanity at all. It was like talking to an animated corpse.'

Jarrett nodded to Tommy Quinn and the latter left the office to pursue this fresh line of enquiry. The odd character may or may not have been involved in the matter to hand, but whatever his game was he had to be taken off the streets as soon as possible. For once, at least, the description was good enough to work on.

The Superintendent leaned back in his chair and tried to come to terms with the fact that the knife-throwing notion seemed to be just another dead end. They were no further on. But at least they hadn't charged Rumsen with anything.

Before sending him on his way, however, Jarrett decided to make absolutely sure that the method of killing had been a straightforward stabbing.

'Tell me,' he said after a few moments, 'would it be possible for you to hit a moving target?'

'A man, you mean? If he was coming at me, yes, but probably not if he was crossing my eyeline.'

'Consider this, Mr Rumsen.' Jarrett selected a sheet of paper and quickly sketched what he believed to be the murder weapon. 'Perhaps nine or ten inches in length, tubular handle, a half inch square blade tapering to a point. Could you throw such a thing?'

'I very much doubt it.' Rumsen replied. 'A

knife rotates in the air, you know. This looks more like a dart.'

'If you had to try, how would you do it?'

'Well, there's the hammer grip, where you hold the handle, or the pinch grip, where you hold the blade. The pinch grip is the fastest delivery, but in my opinion neither method would be any use with your object, whatever it is.'

'Why?'

'The blade is as wrong as it can be. If you wanted to kill a man who was wearing a coat, waistcoat and shirt you would need a knife that was both heavy and razor-sharp. You would be better with a knitting needle than this thing.'

Charlie Grant's theory was now dead and buried, and all that was left was to see that John Harold Rumsen was safely returned to Edinburgh. Happily, there seemed to be no hard feelings on his part, and perhaps even a touch of pride at being able in some small measure to assist the police.

Some fifteen or so minutes after Inspector Grant and the pleasant Mr Rumsen had departed for Queen's Street Station — the latter having declined the offer of a hotel room at the city's expense, because he wanted to make sure that his horse and van were quite safe — Sergeant Quinn returned from

Records and presented Henry Jarrett with a sheet. There was even a photograph clipped to it. It was just as the knife-thrower had said. The eyes were so pale they could scarcely be seen.

'Lawrence William Short,' he said. 'Released from the Royal Lunatic Asylum two weeks ago after serving fifteen years for drowning his wife, Mary, in her zinc tub. Apparently he effected this by simply pulling her feet up in the air until all signs of life had ceased, then tried to make out that he had found her dead. They didn't accept it. He was nicknamed the Bathtub Killer, and the prosecution wanted him to hang, but Short's defence council argued that she had driven him insane with her constant bleating about money. There was no insurance claim involved, or he certainly would have got the rope.'

'Presumably he has been judged sane enough to be put back into the swim,' Jarrett observed.

'It wouldn't be the first time they've got it wrong. Trying to hire a killer isn't exactly the act of a sane man, especially not in such a public place.'

'I couldn't agree with you more.' The superintendent returned the sheet and picture to Quinn. 'Ideally we should pull him out of circulation, but I don't think that's going to be easy. This is a big city and we only have limited resources.'

'What do you suggest, sir?'

'Find out all you can about the original case. Get a list of everyone involved, no matter how peripherally. Of course, he might be seeking revenge on just about anyone for just about any reason, but the greater likelihood is that the intended target had something to do with his downfall fifteen years ago.'

* * *

For the second evening running, Henry Jarrett got back to 76 Delmont Avenue at a decent hour. The other three gentlemen guests had finished their evening meal and retired to their respective rooms, but since Mrs Maitland had not received notification that he would be unduly late, she had kept a decent portion of rump steak, mashed potatoes and broccoli low down in the oven and hoped for the best. The hot water would not be added to the Black Dragon tea until he actually stepped over the threshold. Stewed Ti Kuan Yin had a bitterness that was not to his liking.

As always when the opportunity for relaxation arose, the superintendent brought the cane chair from the corner of his room and placed it squarely in front of the Wardian case to let his thoughts run free in the fern forest. The pottery fisherman was still having no luck, but in that he was not entirely alone. Too many cul-de-sacs, too many fruitless notions, too much confusion and nothing to show for it. If Jarrett could have changed places with the little fellow at that precise moment of time he would happily have done so.

For some reason he couldn't quite put his finger on, his thoughts now centred on the one who had persuaded the lunacy panel that he was now as sane as they were. Considering their decision this might well have been the case.

Trouble was, the Canadian case and the lunatic ought to have received equal weight because both probably involved the prevention of yet another untimely death. There had been no mention of Lorimer since he tricked his way into Mrs MacNiven's house, so it was not impossible that he was lying somewhere with a small square hole in his chest and nothing in his pockets. But if not, then every effort should be made to find him and extend the protection of the law. Criminal or not, he had the right to life.

But there was also the slight matter of the

avenging madman, the one dubbed the Bathtub Killer. His proposed victim, whoever he or she was, equally deserved to be located and protected, at least until Lawrence William Short had been returned to the Royal Lunatic Asylum, this time for the remainder of his life. Trying to buy the services of a killer ought to be more than sufficient to ensure that.

The girl, Lizzie, was also in his thoughts. Elsie Maitland had joined him for a short time after he had finished his dinner and expressed her concern that the maid was still not herself. Normally a bright, quick girl, she was still brooding under a dark cloud of silence. In Mrs Maitland's opinion, Lizzie was far too young to have become a depressive, and anyway there could have been no outside influence to bring it on. She worked, as any God-fearing girl should, from six o'clock in the morning until she was no longer required in the evening, and had only her half-day per fortnight in which to visit her mother. What could possibly have happened, Elsie wondered, to change her from her cheery self to a dark and sullen shadow?

This little discussion, Jarrett thought later, revealed more about the good Mrs Maitland than Lizzie Gill. Many a mistress of the house would have merely told the girl to buck up or be gone, since her demeanour scarcely contributed to the general warmth and goodwill expected by a superior class of paying guest. Elsie Maitland's caring attitude, then, said a great deal for her and would have set her up another notch in the opinion of Superintendent Henry Jarrett, were it not for the fact that she already occupied the topmost position. There was no lady in all the world whose possessions he would rather merge with his.

⋆ ⋆ ⋆

The one they called the Bathtub Killer had his very own nightmare. It had grown over the years from the day they put him in a straightjacket, despite his screams and protestations that he could not stand having his limbs restricted. All of his life until that moment seemed to have been devoted to the terror of being buried alive. But he always assumed that it would be in the cold ground. When it came it was in the form of a canvas jacket, strapped and buckled, and a darkened room in a tiled asylum full of howls and echoes. He couldn't move, shriek or scratch himself. Before they released him he was no longer faking. He was mad.

Every night thereafter the same monstrous

nightmare. The thing that pressed on the right side of his twisted head and on his chest and knees was solid, immovable. And he was cold. He slowly clenched his fingers and felt them biting into smooth clay, then twisted his hands at the wrists and touched the unyielding surface above — wood, grainy, rough-hewn. He lowered his hands again and patted the sides of his prison with splayed fingers. He was going to panic. There was nothing he could do about it, for all the dread of years had not prepared him for a moment like this.

Everything had been swept aside to make room for him. His left hand explored the disjointed bones as the index and middle fingers of his right curled into the eye sockets of the skull.

He was screaming in the pitch and frozen blackness.

Then he was sitting bolt upright, sweating profusely and screaming until all the others joined in.

The room he now paid three shillings a week for in Clyde Loan was spartan, but sufficient. When he ate, it was just enough to stave off the hunger that interfered with his endless planning. And he only drank water, because alcohol led to overconfidence and mistakes.

It was not too difficult to keep his thoughts fixed on what he had to do, since on the rare occasions when he had tried to recall the better times the urgency and power of his driving vengeance would push such trifling nonsense out of his mind, until all that remained were the faces and the names. And one name, one face in particular. It was the man who, more than any other, had contributed to his torture.

There was a thick sandwich of brown bread and cheese left over from earlier in the day. He seated himself at the small table, placed his palms on the underside of the wooden surface and closed his eyes. The nightmare had become real now. He could actually feel the awful crushing on his cheekbone and ribs and knees, the dreadful terror of being unable to move his feet because they protruded from under the covering plank and were buried in the clay, the hideous realization that he had been buried alive, and within his head he could hear the screaming that was never going to end.

He could contemplate only one task at a time. The first had to be the one who gave him the name, the Bathtub Killer, and opened the floodgates of brutality and hatred that are always reserved for those who are different, those who have strange identities.

Because of the name he had been bullied and brutalized.

The attempt at hiring a knifeman to do his dirty work for him had been a bad mistake. He knew that the moment he saw the look in the showman's eyes. As an idea in the middle of a sleepless night it had seemed quite clever and even flawless. He would get an expert to do the job, then he would kill the expert, leaving nothing whatsoever to connect him with the deed. In the cold light of day, however, the plan turned out to be no plan at all. Unless he was a complete fool, the rogue would demand the money in advance and almost certainly run off with it. And anyway, where would he find two hundred pounds? He might as well have offered the man a thousand or a million. He only had a sovereign and some scrap.

He had to attend to it in person, and it must be straightforward, unannounced and swift. No more foolish and intricate schemes which, as a result of being unduly convoluted, would almost certainly come apart at the joins as soon as they were implemented. An adult male in good health must be killed quickly, or he may turn the tables on his assailant, and that would not be to the liking of Lawrence William Short. And anyway, he had to see to number one before turning his attention to the second name on his list.

He suddenly thought of warder Harris. There was no particular reason why he should be third or fourth or indeed any number, just as long as he was attended to at some time. It was Harris who showed him the straightjacket and taunted him with it, lapping up every moment of his terror and ignoring his pleas. It was Harris who punched him in the belly and threw him down the stairs, then kicked him repeatedly when he could not get up. But, for now, Harris would keep.

9

They met at 8 a.m. in Jarrett's office to share Sergeant Quinn's findings and to allocate tasks.

'Archives, sir,' Tommy Quinn said, placing his notes on the desk. 'The case against Lawrence William Short for the murder of his wife, Mary Short, was heard in the Glasgow High Court in August 1847. As you know he was found guilty and sentenced to be detained during Her Majesty's Pleasure, which in the event turned out to be a little under fifteen years.

'Here we have the main people involved. Judge Obadiah Bain, now deceased . . . '

'Deceased how?' Jarrett interrupted.

'Old age, sir. Fell to bits.'

'Right, proceed.'

'Obviously, there was the jury, unknown to the defendant. The case was handled by Inspector James Barrowman, also deceased. I understand he died after falling from a factory roof in Finnieston. He was chasing a suspect at the time. And before you ask, sir, it was nine years ago, so Short could have had nothing to do with it.

'Barrowman's team consisted of Detective Sergeant William Tassie, who later emigrated to New Zealand, and one Detective Constable Charles Grant.'

'Really?' Jarrett turned to peer at Charlie Grant for a few moments. 'Seems to have done all right for himself, this DC.'

'Still got the same boots,' Grant said, grinning.

'Short's defence counsel was Mr Thomas Coleman,' Quinn continued, 'and he was prosecuted by Mr David Squires. Both are still to the fore. We also have sundry court officials, who might be identified with a bit of effort, sir.'

'Is that all?'

'Apart from one Norman Leckie, a neighbour of Short's in Springfield Road. It was really Leckie's account of life in the Short household that both convicted Short and at the same time saved him from the gallows. According to Leckie, who was a foreman at the same Hill and Muir Calico Printing Works that Short worked for, the accused and his wife were forever quarrelling over money, or the lack of it. Mrs Short, Leckie said, wanted the better things in life.'

'Where is Leckie now?'

'Pushing up the daisies, I'm afraid.' Tommy Quinn shrugged lightly. 'Would you like me to try to find a living neighbour?'

'No, I shouldn't think that's necessary.' Henry Jarrett leaned back and thought about Elsie Maitland. There were not many women in their early forties who did not require a corset in order to keep a sylph-like form. The great secret, which most cooks tended to ignore, was not to be one's own best customer. The late Mr Maitland, it seemed, had gorged for both of them, and for that Henry Jarrett was most grateful. 'So, who do we have? Inspector Grant, Mr Thomas Coleman and Mr David Squires.'

'I'm afraid so, sir.'

'Excuse me for being unduly dense,' Charlie Grant put in, 'but are we pursuing the well-worn path of prisoners' revenge? There hasn't been a convict yet who didn't plot the destruction of those who sent him away. They never see it through, you know.'

'This one isn't a convict, Inspector, he's a madman, and he might very well see it through.' Jarrett turned again to Tommy Quinn. 'As a point of interest, how was he caught?'

'I'm not sure that's the right way to put it, sir,' Quinn replied. 'As soon as he drowned her, he ran for the police and reported the so-called accident.'

'They usually do.' Jarrett clasped his hands

on the large desk blotter and feigned deep thought. Actually, he had already made his mind up about how things should go from now on. 'Two cases of similar import, gentlemen, so I suggest we divide our resources. Inspector Grant, you will concentrate on locating Lawrence Short and nothing else. Sergeant Quinn and I will pursue the Canadian problem and hopefully trace Lorimer before it is too late.'

* * *

The *Advertiser* was Peter McGovern's life. It took the place of a wife, children and even friends. In fact, he never could see much point in the latter. People were on earth to be used. They either committed some felony that was worth writing about, or they were the newspaper-buying public who thirsted for the salacious details he supplied. Murder, thievery, naked women, adultery and rape made him sit up and listen. This time Jimmy Lyle hit him with two out of the five. He had the naked women and the adultery.

'You've got to get in there, Jimmy,' McGovern ordered. 'We both know you could write the piece without ever leaving the office, but this time I want to know who is really there.'

Lyle nodded, pleased with himself. For once, the editor was setting his sights higher than his usual dirty romps. These were big people. This was politics and had the potential to be very dangerous indeed. But Peter McGovern had the guts to go all out for it. Shit or burst.

'Are you going to name them?' Lyle asked.

'Sir L or Mrs T is good enough. The public can fill in the missing letters as quickly as you could scratch your arse. And the nobs know it. Their strong sense of position and self-preservation won't allow it to happen.'

Jimmy Lyle grinned broadly. The grizzled old bugger would blackmail Jesus if he could get something on him. What he had in mind this time was highly questionable and only marginally legal. He would present each of the identified ones with a copy of the piece for comment and give them a deadline for publication. The foolish ones would serve him with a writ; the smart ones would take out full-page advertisements if they were in business, or make a healthy donation to whichever charity McGovern favoured if they were landed gentry. But that apart, it would be very nice to have a list of those and such as those who could be called upon at some time in the future to assist in delicate matters. The article itself would never appear. It wasn't meant to.

'I'll need a letter from you authorizing the investigation into this lapse of morals among the great and the good,' Lyle said flatly. 'I could get five years in Duke Street Prison for breaking and entering a mansion.'

McGovern frowned at this. Blackmailing others was acceptable, but being blackmailed was intolerable. In the end, of course, there was nothing for it but to comply. He wanted the real names, not some tripe Lyle had concocted while waiting for a result in the privy.

'You'll get it,' he grumbled.

'Signed by you.'

Peter McGovern reached for a sheet of his precious writing paper, impatiently dabbed his pen into the inkwell and proceeded to scrawl an editorial absolution.

'Ideally, don't get caught. It would seriously jeopardize what I have in mind.'

Lyle quickly scanned the blotted sheet, then folded it twice and put it away in his inside pocket. Just how much it would help in an awkward situation was anybody's guess.

'Would you like a couple of half-plates?' he asked. He was only half joking. 'They will be arriving before eight, so there will still be an hour or two of daylight.'

McGovern shook his head adamantly.

'Definitely not. A photograph of some nob arriving at a big house in his landau would prove absolutely nothing. Just see how many faces you can put a name to and, if you can gain access to the mansion, try to capture the essence of the whole thing. If you can't, well you're big and ugly enough to imagine a regiment of bare bums and tits writhing on the dancehall floor, but I would rather you were an eyewitness who could swear on the Bible. If you can't tell them apart, just say that Lord B was stoking Mrs G's boiler. They're hardly going to dispute it, are they? I mean, they're all going to be wearing papier-mâché masks, for Christ's sake, so the dirty buggers won't know who they've jumped on.'

Jimmy Lyle couldn't help feeling that McGovern's words revealed more than just a shade of jealousy as he quit the office and made his way down the staircase to the greater world and whatever passed for fresh air.

⋆ ⋆ ⋆

Charlie Grant paused briefly at the corner of Woodhill Terrace and Hawthorn Avenue to collect his thoughts. Since Short's file had last been updated Mr David Squires had joined the great majority and Mr Thomas Coleman had retired to Largs, where he no doubt spent his time ruminating and gazing out over the Firth of Clyde. Question was, could Lawrence William Short find this out? Would a released inmate with little or no resources have access to that sort of information, or any information at all? Where would he go? Who would he ask? More to the point, who would entrust him with such sensitive details as the private addresses of prominent people? In the end the inspector decided that it would be virtually impossible for Short to find out anything.

But he could quite easily follow Charlie Grant and that was disconcerting. More than once he had stopped and taken a surreptitious look over his shoulder, and each time felt rather foolish for doing so. At the same time he had to admit that the threat of menace was not entirely unwelcome, like a maiden lady half-dreading, half-hoping there was someone hiding under the bed.

Considering the size of the city compared to the size of his feet, an attempted attack by Short resulting in his immediate capture and internment would be the best solution, if not the only one. Truth was, Grant had no idea where to begin. Although the Ticket of Leave system was supposed to record the whereabouts of released offenders it was wide open to abuse. The temporary address Charlie Grant had for Short turned out to be a gap between two warehouses. The man might be anywhere by now.

55a Woodhill Terrace was something of a long shot. Short's sister, Mrs Davina Thorburn, resided there at the time of the murder and trial, but that was a long time ago and she might be in Heaven by now if she was lucky or the poorhouse if she wasn't. Actually, it was neither. She was still *in situ*, but widowed now and still in support of her brother. Since she didn't remember the younger Charlie Grant and probably had no real reason to do so, he thought it best not to refresh her memory.

Having made the tea and buttered the scones, Mrs Thorburn took her place on the other side of the top-tilt coffee table and peered at the inspector.

'I have no idea where Lawrence is,' she said firmly. 'Why would you wish to know, Inspector? Surely he has served more than sufficient time in that place, particularly as he was wholly innocent of the crime. I would have thought that the least the police could do would be to leave him alone to enjoy his remaining years.'

'I wish that were possible, madam,' Grant said, 'but I'm afraid he may be actively seeking revenge.'

'On whom? And for that matter how could you possibly know that?'

'I am not at liberty to say how we know, but it is fairly certain that your brother is out to avenge wrongs committed against him, real or imagined.'

'I hardly think he needs to imagine anything. He suffered more in that asylum than anyone should have to endure in ten lifetimes.'

Grant could see that he would have to choose his words carefully when dealing with this woman, because she seemed to be waiting for any opportunity to strike out in defence of Lawrence William Short. Or maybe she was like that with everything and everyone. It might just have been her way.

'You visited him when he was in — '

'The lunatic asylum, yes.' Davina Thorburn stared at him as though trying to get into his thoughts and, for all he knew, influence them. Yet he had to be grateful to the woman for finishing his sentence for him. It was not the word he was going to use. She continued, 'The last Friday in every month.'

'Did he ever say anything to you about

feeling unduly bitter towards anyone in particular?'

'I wouldn't say unduly, Inspector. I would say justifiably.'

He nodded thoughtfully and for a moment was tempted to ask how her husband had died. It wouldn't have surprised him in the slightest to discover that it involved a zinc bath.

'I understand how upsetting for you this must be, Mrs Thorburn,' he said, but somehow it lacked sincerity, 'but it is essential that we talk to your brother, if only to satisfy ourselves that everything is all right.'

'I am sorry I can't help you,' the widow replied flatly. 'We agreed that it might not be wise for him to call here.'

'But surely you arranged to see him after his release.'

'No. He was the one who decided against that. We both knew that his health was deteriorating and he had no wish to be a burden on me, especially not after the years of trouble I had with my late husband.' Mrs Thorburn continued to eye him accusingly as she added, 'I thought it was compulsory for him to leave his address with his local police station.'

'It was false.' Grant allowed this to sink in. 'Giving the police deliberately erroneous information is hardly conducive to creating a bond of trust. Put another way, Madam, your brother got off to a very bad start in his new life.'

'I doubt if Lawrence has much of a life to look forward to. If you had seen him before he was falsely incriminated in the death of that woman you would be appalled by the change. He isn't just fifteen years older, Inspector, he is a different person.'

'Do I take it that you didn't hold Mrs Short in high regard?'

'I didn't have any regard for her. To say that I held her in low esteem would be to flatter her. After giving him a dog's life, she even managed to reach out from beyond the grave and finish him off.'

'You don't believe it was murder?'

Mrs Thorburn gave a sharp laugh.

'Oh, it was murder, all right, but Lawrence didn't do it.'

'Then who did?'

'There is only one person with cause and opportunity, Inspector,' she said, 'and that was Norman Leckie, the neighbour whose so-called evidence put Lawrence in the madhouse.'

'Why should Leckie have killed Mary Short?'

'Because she was no better than she ought

to be, that's why. It's my opinion that she threatened to tell his wife about this and that, so he had no choice but to dispatch her.' Mrs Thorburn reached for the teapot, but Charlie Grant declined the offer of a refill by covering his cup with a palm. 'It would have been the easiest thing for him to drown her while Lawrence was outside in the privy. After all, her door was always open.'

'Even when she was in her bath?'

'I would have thought especially then. As I said, no better than she ought to be.'

And that, mused Charlie Grant, was the damnedest thing. At the time he had mentioned the fact to Sergeant Tassie and Inspector Barrowman that he didn't believe Short to be guilty, but Barrowman waved his opinions aside because he had the husband very firmly in his sights. Anyway, what did a bloody constable know? Couldn't find his arse with a map.

But the fact that Short may have been innocent of his wife's murder altered nothing: he was still hell-bent on revenge and for that reason alone had to be caught.

When Grant left the house at 55a Woodhill Terrace it was with the reinforced conviction that Short was innocent of the murder of his wife. He was equally convinced that Mrs Thorburn was lying when she said that there had been no connection with Short since his release. The man had to be living on something, so he was being fed at the very least. The only person who would do that was his sister.

But he certainly did believe her when she told him that Short had been discouraged from coming to her home. The reason for that was not hard to find and had little to do with what the neighbours thought. More likely, Grant thought, the woman was capable of sound reasoning even if what remained of Lawrence Short was not. She would know instinctively that this would be the first place the police would raid, and that in turn suggested that Davina Thorburn knew about the proposed righting of wrongs.

But first things first. Sooner or later the devoted Mrs Thorburn would leave Woodhill Terrace for parts unknown and when that happened she would be followed every step of the way.

Just around the corner in Hawthorn Avenue one of the rear doors of a carrier's wagon swung open and Charlie Grant jumped inside. Detective Sergeant Morrison, newly up from the ranks, was stuffing his face with two large slices of bread wrapped round a half cow.

'She's in it, all right,' the inspector said, rubbing his hands. 'What's for eating?'

* * *

If the woods around Yorkhill House provided a measure of seclusion, the veritable forest encircling Darnwood Mansion was clearly intended to deter all but the most determined. Although it was July and the evening sun was still very much in evidence in a clear sky, Jimmy Lyle had taken the precaution of adding an extra layer of wool next to his immediate person, and decided at the last moment to bring along his three-quarter coat just in case the temperature suddenly took a downward turn. From long experience he knew that the enforced immobility of surveillance led to rapid loss of body heat, so he also brought a canvas bag with cheese, ham and a flask of brandy.

Between Lyle and the front of the estate house was a wide front lawn and at least sixty feet of loose gravel chippings, the latter shifting and grinding beneath the iron-rimmed wheels of a fleet of expensive carriages. As he watched, a good two dozen open phaetons, briskas and landaus, along with cabbed and enclosed broughams, clarences and barouches, disgorged their human occupants before setting off once more down the long driveway. For thirty minutes or more, the scrunching of boots and bootees on the wide forecourt competed with hearty greetings and the neighing of fine horses, while Jimmy Lyle, armed with opera glasses, notepad and a pocketful of pencil stubs, swiftly recorded the names of all he knew by sight and made a few good guesses as to who the rest were. Sometimes the vehicles gave the game away, particularly as the prevailing colours were dictated by the escutcheons of the greater families. The only colour missing was scarlet. There was no Royalty.

The quality of the coachmen and their underlings also helped to put names to faces. All stable staff, whatever the position, were permitted sideburns, but never moustaches or beards. This to differentiate between the servant and his master, who frequently preferred full face furniture. The waistcoats of all coach and stable servants, whatever the social position of their betters, carried horizontal stripes. Indoor staff had vertical stripes. But it was the style and cut of their coats, gloves and boots that often marked them out as special.

In his own way, Lyle was a student of human nature. That made him more of an authority on these people and their motives than they were themselves. Not all of them were driven to this place by the lust of the loins. In some cases it was cold, calculated ambition, or response to a piece of advice, usually accompanied by a wink and a nod. These people would probably not participate in the coming free for all, but would see to their business and quietly depart. This evening, there were three such arrangements being attended to, and he could tell this by the three cabs that were still waiting after the others had departed. Without exception, they were from the cheaper end of the market — first vehicles of those ascending the social or professional ladder. Lyle bit off another lump of cheese and stuck the remainder back into his canvas bag. These special agreements never were particularly prolonged, so he shouldn't have to wait too long, he thought, just long enough for the ambitious young wives to get their clothes back on.

He had spent a large part of the afternoon figuring out how best to approach the mansion, and had ruled out any attempt at crossing the large expanse of loose gravel. While he waited for the three couples who had elevated themselves a little more this evening to hurry out, climb into their carriages and quit the place, he double-checked his final plan. Unlike Yorkhill House, the square in front of the stables offered no place to hide. The east wing of the mansion overlooked that completely. And the rear of the entire edifice was one huge garden, taken up with glasshouses, vegetable patches and an abundance of obstacles barring a direct route to the back door. Anyway, the kitchen would be in turmoil right then, so while it could provide a means of entering the house without being noticed by the flustered staff, it might equally present him with numerous opportunities for being challenged. This would be almost certain if the housekeeper was supervising the preparations.

That left only the west wing, with its enormous conservatory. If the large glazed door was not still open, several of the sloping windows would be. The prevailing attitude among the toffs was that burglars would think twice before tackling a small army of footmen, many of whom had seen military service. Also, stealing from the wealthy was roundly punished, and although it was rarely used now transportation to Australia was still an option open to the courts in defence of superiority and privilege. A cover note from Peter McGovern could make all the difference.

But before he could approach the conservatory, Lyle would have to negotiate the thick woods and reach the old burial ground. When the last of the three ambitious couples had driven off, no doubt convinced that they had taken advantage of the mighty and the lecherous, who probably felt exactly the same way about them, Lyle set off to skirt some trees and bounce off others until he reached the fenced cemetery, with its various mausoleums of the different families who had owned the mansion. There he paused to consider exactly what he was going to do and how he was going to do it.

It was ten long yards from the edge of the trees to the ornate iron fence. Lyle took it in the same number of paces, pressed himself against the cold metal for a few moments, then scurried across the untended grassland and once more squatted, braced, against the brick foundation of the large glass construction. The interior of the conservatory was filled with palms and other greenery, but little in the way of flowers. It was completely impossible to say for certain that no humans were indulging themselves within.

To his great relief he found that the present owners of the estate had put all their faith in God and the courts, thus sparing him the task of clambering through a partly open window and perhaps cutting his throat in the process. The large brass catch yielded under his thumb and the door slowly opened onto a warm and luxuriant world, a tropical world, where leaning palm trees twice the height of himself formed a rich green canopy and heavy flagstone pathways curved right and left, only to take the feet back to where they started. By such a clever use of twists and turns a maze-like jungle had been created that seemed to be many times larger than it really was.

A second door at the inner end of the conservatory led to a narrow hallway and onward to three other doors, each of which opened on to three small rooms, the first packed with miscellaneous boxes and the others with sundry bits and pieces which seemed in some sense connected to the conservatory. At this point he had to decide whether to go right or left along the rather tight and constricted passage, but although he could hear the hum of distant babble it was impossible to pinpoint its source. From the very beginning, he had been certain of only one thing: he wasn't going to get away with it for long and that any moment he was going to have to make a run for it. Hopefully, that would be after he had satisfied himself that this gathering was exactly what the stable boy assured him it would be, and not some wholly innocent soirée that could fetch McGovern and the paper into court to face a wheelbarrowful of defamation claims.

It was also true to say that he wasn't exactly averse to seeing fancy ladies in their underwear or less. The women he associated with when he got his wages on Saturday night didn't wear drawers. He had always felt that it was grossly unfair that the absence of them could get a girl arrested and hauled up before the beak in the morning, charged with running her business from on the flagstones. It was quite interesting to speculate on exactly how the beat coppers found out, and what might happen if they were wrong. It would serve the buggers right, he thought.

Up until this moment he had been too busy to feel nervous or threatened, but now his stomach began to turn over and a herd of butterflies all took to the air at once. It wouldn't have taken much to send him scurrying back through the conservatory and across the grass to the safety of the trees. Then a door far to the left of him creaked open and he found himself inside the nearest room, crouching, holding the doorknob and his breath.

Lyle squatted there, listening to the approaching footsteps and praying that this was not the man's intended destination. That it was a man left him in no doubt. The steps were heavy and measured, and although it was just barely possible that it was a dwarf with enormous feet, his luck just didn't work that way.

What happened next was the closest thing to actually having his collar felt by a pig, or *chazer* as the Hebrews would say. The inner door to the conservatory squeaked, the long tackety bootsteps echoed on the winding flagstones and a chunky-sounding key secured the outer door for the night. When the whole process was again played out in reverse and the man had once more disappeared into the guts of the building itself, Jimmy Lyle had no way out.

After a few minutes the panic subsided and he was again capable of rational thought, or as close to it as he ever was. He was now in the position of having to brazen it out, and the best way to do that would be to walk swiftly and confidently through the kitchens and out into the evening air. He rose to his full height, which was never great at the best of times, pulled open the door and strode along the narrow corridor in the direction of God knows what. His instinct told him that this had been a bad mistake, and that the best thing he could do was get to hell out of there. It wasn't too much to ask for.

Taking pot luck, he pulled open the closest door and found himself in another store and confronted by an array of weird and wonderful faces. Devils, lions and a variety of demi-creatures with hollow, empty eyeholes were displayed on shelves, but whether these were the ones required for the festivities or those no one wanted was impossible to say.

Since this was the last room, Lyle retraced his steps and made for the green door at the other end of the corridor. He opened it cautiously and found himself in yet another passageway, this time richer and fully carpeted. The walls were of cherry-red flock and gas lights hung from chains attached to large plaster roses on the ornate ceiling.

One of the glossy red doors was carelessly ajar, and the sounds that came from within were not those normally associated with gracious living. They were the unashamed noises of the farmyard mingled with the brazen thudding and twanging of a large, ill-treated bed. Being human and making no apologies for it, Lyle paused briefly at the slightly open door and told himself that he was really trying to identify the participants, and not a mere voyeur relishing nude intercourse between a mismatched pair. The lady was young and not entirely naked. Her white cotton stockings were secured above the knees by bow-tied satin garters and she had tiny bows in her hair. The man was as bare as a fuzzy peach and old enough to be her father at the very least. Everything about the scene smacked of the exploitation of privilege. The young wife wanted to exchange her cotton stockings for silk ones and could only do that by pushing her husband up the ladder of success. In Jimmy Lyle's long experience of both sides of human nature — bad and worse — whenever man acquired the power to demand favours he saw lesser men's wives as his personal playthings.

Lyle moved on then, this time in the direction of a large, leather padded and studded door, but was even more wary now and ready for any sudden confrontation. He had no way of knowing how many of these rooms were occupied or when a door might suddenly be thrown open, leaving him in the invidious position of having to explain why a middle-aged, fully clothed man with a pair of binoculars and a notebook was strolling through the house in search of an orgy.

When he reached the door unchallenged, he waited for a few moments before taking hold of the large brass knob. Muffled laughter, raucous and coarse, and high-pitched squeals of delight encouraged him to investigate further, but a fear of what lay on the other side served to stay his hand. How many were in there, and were they at a safe distance, or would he walk in upon the merrymaking with no excuse for his uninvited presence and no way out? Since there was nothing else for it, he gently turned the knob and drew the door open just enough to see what he was letting himself in for.

He had imagined a situation in which forty or fifty naked revellers, each retaining his or her anonymity behind a mask, writhed like pink eels on an enormous carpet, entwined and copulating with everyone and anyone. Perhaps that was how it had been a few minutes ago, when it all began, but it now seemed that more than just a few had rapidly burned themselves out and failed to live up to their desires and expectations. These ones had largely discarded their masks and now lounged on piles of scattered cushions, drinking and watching those whose libidos permitted them to stay the distance. Even most of those who provided the spectacle had required the papier-mâché masks only during the initial insecure stage and had soon cast them aside.

Lyle slowly sank to his knees, pulled back the door another few inches, crawled into the ballroom and positioned himself behind one of the large columns. From there he could see that such sofas and chairs that might be found on the periphery of the dancing area had been pushed back into the shadows. The wall lamps had been turned down to a mere glow and all but one of the large hanging gaslights had been turned off. The sexual survivors whose thrusting and writhing provided a visual feast for those who had retired from the competition were rapidly becoming fewer in number as one by one the exhausted males crawled over to the drinks trays. After a little refreshment, perhaps, they might resume their valiant efforts. But Jimmy Lyle would not be around to confirm that.

There was a sudden movement behind him and he turned abruptly to confront three large, colourful masks, all garish and all devils. But the eyeholes were no longer dark and void like the ones in the store: these ones were staring at him.

⋆ ⋆ ⋆

Henry Jarrett was just about to call it a day when Sergeant Quinn arrived in the office with his latest find. At least there would be something to justify getting up that morning. Some days, the superintendent decided, just begged to have a red line put through them.

'A few moments, sir,' Quinn said hurriedly, dumping a pile of discoloured newspapers on the desk. 'These are from the day Short was found guilty, 23 June 1847.'

Jarrett hung his coat back onto the deerhorn and returned to his seat. Something in Tommy Quinn's expression told him that it might be worthwhile.

'Surely this is Inspector Grant's area of operations,' he said, yet he couldn't hide his interest.

'Indeed it is, Superintendent, but I couldn't get rid of the idea that I may have overlooked someone.'

'Proceed, Sergeant,' he said.

Quinn spread the papers out and indicated each one in turn.

' 'Short guilty', 'Short Insane', 'Short is Mad', 'Short Guilty but Insane', 'The Bathtub Killer Insane'.' The sergeant tapped the final paper with a stiff index finger. 'The work of our old friend, Jimmy Lyle, who spends his life pestering the desk sergeant for tips — when he isn't hanging around the mortuary, that is.'

Superintendent Jarrett sat forward and clasped his hands on the blotter.

'There's more,' he said. 'I can tell.'

'Yes, sir, there's more. Short's sister, Mrs Davina Thorburn, wrote to the *Advertiser* on numerous occasions, complaining about his grim treatment and blaming Lyle for having branded him this way. In one particular letter she even went as far as saying that Lyle would pay for his crime, however long it took. That, I gather, was the proverbial straw that broke the camel's back. The editor reported the matter to the Constabulary and Mrs Thorburn received a visit and a warning. There were no more letters after that.'

'But that doesn't mean the hatred ceased.'

'By no means, sir. If Short really is insane official action like that would only have strengthened his belief that the whole world was on one side of the chalk line and he was on the other.' Quinn collected the papers and tucked them under his arm. 'It's Lyle he's after; I'm sure of it.'

'Where is Inspector Grant now?'

The sergeant shrugged lightly.

'Out and about, sir.'

'Well, make sure he gets that information when he returns.' Jarrett's spirits had risen in the last few minutes. A positive development was always welcome. 'If anything further transpires you know where to find me. It's hazelhen pot roast tonight.'

'Don't miss it, sir.'

'Absolutely no intention of.'

* * *

As Jimmy Lyle stumbled along the moonlit path, breathless from enforced exertion but grateful to have got off with a mere threat or two and a rough exit out into the stable yard, the silhouettes of large houses came and went. But he did not see them. Nor did he see the dark river or the clumps of reed along its banks.

It was clear even to his fear-muddled brain that they had let him go only because they did not wish to attract attention to the mansion and its shenanigans. Otherwise they would almost certainly have sent for the law and had him prosecuted, or tried to. Of course, McGovern's untried and untested letter might have won the day, but he was loath to put it to the test. That was why he didn't produce it, and since they made no attempt to search him it still nestled in his inner pocket.

At first he thought the thing was a huge dog. He stopped, and since there was nothing else for it, remained where he was, his eyes fixed on the large shape as it moved through the moon shadows some way to the left of him, passing him, getting between him and his destination.

Not unnaturally, this cautiousness on its part suggested that the creature was more afraid than he was, and it gave him confidence to continue. He would dismiss all foolish fears, he decided, and hopefully drive the beast in front of him. After all, he was a man, while it was a mere creature.

But it would not be driven. Now that it had reached the well-trodden path it crouched in the thick shadow by a bunch of tall reeds and let him come as close as he thought prudent. Then it stood up.

One fist gripped the front of his coat; the other was over his eyes, pressing his head backwards and reducing his whimpering to a choking hiss. The river-bank crumbled and cold water swept around his legs. Then his knees buckled under the force and only his face and clawing hands showed above the surface.

He tried to scream but the sudden chill had driven much of the air from his lungs, so that it came out as a coarse wheeze. Now the water was everywhere. It saturated every thread of clothing on his body. It was in his throat, his nose and his ears, causing him to struggle as he had never struggled before. But in the end he lacked the strength to deny his attacker the ultimate satisfaction.

One minute . . . two . . . then the bubbles stopped. Jimmy Lyle was dead.

10

Aggie Tait had faithfully scrubbed the wooden stair in the Kelvin Bakeries just after dawn every morning for the last five years, which suited night-watchman Ted MacStay down to the ground. Mrs Tait might not be a fashion follower, and she would certainly never see forty again, but she had a way of swinging her rump while she scrubbed that put lead in his pencil, and not many were able to do that now. It was his great delight to quit his stool to go and sit behind her on the lower steps where he could tell her the sort of jokes she liked to hear and which did her most good, especially when Mr Tait was at sea.

Unfortunately, on that particular occasion it seemed that the good lady's husband was firmly entrenched at home and making full use of the amenities, because she was in no mood for MacStay's coarse humour.

She and her bucket had no sooner ascended the creaky staircase to the second landing that she was back down in the foyer again.

'Here,' she whispered, 'I've just been looking out of the window. I think there's someone in the water.'

'Never. There was nothing there when I did my rounds.' MacStay rose from his stool in the alcove and collected his knobbly stick from the shelf where he kept his bits and pieces. 'You're probably seeing things. Gone scrubbing crazy, like what happens to them in jail.'

'I've done no such thing,' she declared softly. 'I know a floater when I see one. And anyway, it could have come down since you were out.'

'Then maybe it has gone on by now.'

'No, looks stuck.'

'Right,' MacStay said, having exhausted his excuses, 'let's go and take a look.'

'No thank you,' replied Aggie Tait, with a pronounced nod. 'I'm just the cleaner. And anyway, it isn't lucky to find dead bodies first thing in the morning.'

'Who said that?'

'I did,' she said.

* * *

It was supposed to be an 8 a.m. meeting to pool findings, but in the event it was dominated by just one incident. Tommy Quinn placed an assortment of items on Jarrett's large blotter and clasped his hands behind his back as was his wont.

'Some of the possessions found on a body taken from the Kelvin at dawn this morning, sir,' he said. 'I have tried to dry them out as best I can, but the letter was written in ink and is almost entirely illegible. The notebook is in pencil and has survived very well. His coat pockets also contained a canvas bag with some food, an assortment of pencil stubs and a pair of opera glasses. And he had just under two pounds in his trouser pocket.'

Jarrett frowned, first at the equally puzzled Charlie Grant, then at young Quinn.

'Am I missing something?' he asked.

'Oh, sorry, sir,' Quinn replied. 'I thought I told you. It is, or was, Jimmy Lyle, that newspaper character who was always hanging about in the entrance.'

'Drunk?'

'I don't think so, Superintendent. In fact, Dr Hamilton would like to talk to you in an hour or so, but I gather that first signs do not point to accidental drowning.'

'Murder?' Charlie Grant asked.

'There are indications, sir, but the glasses and money seem to rule out robbery as a motive.' Quinn gave Charlie Grant an apologetic smile. 'I'd say we all know who is at the head of the list if it does turn out to be a deliberate killing.'

'Perhaps.' Henry Jarrett sat heavily in his large, padded chair and looked decidedly concerned. He reached over, snatched up the letter which he almost immediately discarded, then settled down to consider the names and details on the still damp notebook. 'Has anyone else seen this, Sergeant?'

'No, sir.'

'Do you know what it is?'

'I know what I think it is.'

Jarrett gave the book to Grant and waited for a reaction.

'Potentially explosive,' the inspector said after a minute or so.

Jarrett took back the notebook, squirrelled it away in a empty desk drawer and turned the key on it.

'I don't want this mentioned to anyone,' he said firmly. 'It might just be in our interests to keep it up the proverbial sleeve until needed.'

'Good idea,' said Grant, 'but how do we approach it?'

'For the time being it is just another floater until it is established that foul play was involved. There is the obvious link between Lyle and the Bathtub Killer, but at the same time we all know the sort of things that go on in Darnwood Mansion. A risk to reputation could provide grounds for murder. Judging by the notebook he got at least as far as watching them arrive, and he might even have tried to gain access to the place.'

'That could be pretty serious,' Charlie Grant observed. 'Murder at that level could prove difficult to investigate.'

'Almost impossible, I would say. That's why it has to look just like any other tragic accident for now.'

Charlie Grant mulled this over.

'Which of us follows it up, Superintendent?' he asked at length.

'Well, the possibility of Short having a hand in it makes it your area of operations, so you stick with that for the time being. As there is also a chance that he might have been caught in Darnwood Mansion and either deliberately or accidentally killed by being thrown into the river, Sergeant Quinn can interview the editor, although that will almost certainly be a waste of time. If he was after a lever to use against the hoity-toity he isn't likely to admit it.' Jarrett directed his full attention to Tommy Quinn. 'He will no doubt try to find out if Lyle's notebook survived, Sergeant. Act daft and deny all knowledge of it.'

* * *

When he first applied to join the Detective Department, Constable Ian Williamson saw himself apprehending killers and acid-throwers, forgers and major villains of all kinds. They did not tell him that he would be counting the metallic clicks of his boot nails on paving stones as he combed the city in search of oddities and perverts, and especially the ones who preyed on the vulnerable. Now he had reached Freeman's Walk, a roofless arcade, if there could be such a thing. It was long and very narrow, and on either side the dark shops were surmounted by offices to the height of three storeys. It was for all the world a canyon in a city, and like all canyons it seemed to threaten ambush from above.

He stopped outside The Sensible Man's Bookshop and Stationer, let his eyes skim over the curling and yellowing broadsheets. In a few brief seconds he learned, not only that the Aborigines of the Americas were descended from the Lost Tribes of Israel, the true Holy Grail was a wooden begging bowl carved by Jesus the carpenter himself, clean living was the only real safeguard, but that no faith should be placed in those charlatans who professed to reach beyond the veil to the world beyond death. He then pushed a long brass handle and entered the dim and uninviting premises.

Not being unduly bookish, the leather and cloth blocks held little attraction for him.

Instead, he focused his attention on the many pamphlets that were laid out on the counter, each one offering advice on moral improvement. As he moved slowly along the shop he was watched unblinkingly by a young assistant with greasy, centre-parted hair and a pronounced Adam's apple.

A few moments later, that same young man was placed in an invidious position when a gentleman entered and silently held out his hand. In his peripheral vision Williamson saw the assistant hesitate, clearly not wishing to surrender the object, yet at the same time lacking the authority to refuse. After a moment or two's dithering, the youth snatched a key from its hook, handed it over and watched the gent scurry along the length of the narrow shop to the beaded curtain on the left of the far wall.

Detective Constable Williamson gave it a full minute then went in after him.

* * *

Doctor Hamilton welcomed Superintendent Jarrett in his usual customary manner.

'Nice change for you,' he said warmly. 'Not a blade this time.'

There hadn't been much to Lyle in life and there was even less in death. Of no great height, wiry, balding and with a silly little moustache that Jarrett supposed would be more of an irritation than an ornament, Jimmy Lyle would never have won a beauty contest. But then, who would?

'I gather you are not happy with the notion of accidental drowning,' he said.

'Not unless he deliberately held himself under water.' Hamilton indicated the faint bruising on the temples and the lower forehead. 'One hand over his eyes to press him under the surface and the other I suppose holding the front of his coat. At least, that's how I would do it.'

'Would it take great strength?'

'No. Very little, in fact. This man was extremely unfit, had a bad heart he probably didn't know about, and was wearing several layers of clothing which would have made it almost impossible for him to get out of the water. A bit like a knight in armour falling into a moat, I would say. If the other party was holding him under rather than trying to pull him out there would be no chance whatsoever of surviving.'

'Could a woman have done it?'

'A child could have done it.' Hamilton crossed to his corner desk and returned with a large, expensively-printed brochure. 'I brought this in for you, Superintendent. I thought I might treat myself to a new cane, but it occurs to me that you might be more interested in the less usual advertisements at the rear of the catalogue.'

* * *

In the room that was spartan, but sufficient, the Bathtub Killer ate just enough to stave off the hunger that interfered with his endless planning. And, as usual, he only drank tea.

The death of the pencil-scratcher, Lyle, had been singularly unsatisfying. He had hoped for so much more than that, but in the end all he was left with was a dim and dismal memory of the man's fingers slipping away from their feeble attempt at grabbing something solid, something that would allow him to survive. He was just a weak and frightened man who never really knew what was happening to him, or why. Even the feet with their worn boots and darned socks had refused to jerk more than a few miserable times. All in all, Lyle was a great disappointment.

The best remedy of all for such frustration was to keep his mind occupied and fixed on what he next had to do. That was not all that difficult, since on the rare occasions when he had tried to recall the better times the urgency and power of his desire for vengeance would push such trifling nonsense out of his mind, until all that remained were the names and faces. Sadly, some were only names, for he had never seen them. The one who was second on his list was such a man. He had the power to make or break, the power to destroy human beings he had never met. A man like that should not be allowed to live a moment longer than was absolutely necessary. Nor would he.

The Bathtub Killer had so many bad memories, so much agony to dwell on as he ate his sandwich and kept an eye on the pot that simmered on the antiquated black stove. It would take hours for the filthy mixture of water and rat poison to stew down to the thick green residue he was waiting for, but in the end it would be well worth it.

* * *

Inspector Jarrett stood at his desk, his knuckles resting heavily on the polished mahogany surface and his gaze fixed on the spread pages of the cane and walking stick manufacturer's brochure Dr Hamilton had given him. Ever since the killing of William Hartman he had been toying on and off with the idea of the weapon being a swordstick, but somehow it just didn't fit. Now he knew for sure that he was looking at the real thing. But it was something he had never heard of before.

Makila. It was under twelve inches in length and made of hard medlar wood. It had a black horn knob and a leather loop for the wrist, and was described as a gentleman's defence cosh. If the user merely wished to discourage a ruffian and send him on his way he would use it as is. But if the attacker was armed and had designs on the gentleman's life, a swift tug on the handle revealed as lethal a concealed blade as Jarrett had ever seen. It was of square section and tapered rapidly to a deadly point. The length of the blade was no more than seven inches.

Tommy Quinn arrived swiftly in response to the recently installed internal belling system, which Jarrett in particular seemed to particularly favour. Although the superintendent was interested to a certain degree in the strawboard box the young sergeant was carrying, he resisted the temptation to enquire about it and concentrated instead on what, to him at least, was of greatest importance at that moment.

'Gorton's,' Jarrett said, pushing the catalogue across the desk. 'It's a Sheffield company. They manufacture blades and also import from abroad. Find out through the telegraph whether they have supplied any shops up here with this object.'

Quinn quickly read the blurb beneath the line drawing.

'Is this it?' he asked. 'Is this the murder weapon?'

'I would say so. I know it's asking a bit much to hope that the man who killed Hartman and Fenton bought this gadget in Glasgow, but if he did it could save us a lot of time and legwork to find out exactly where.'

'I shouldn't imagine they sell a lot of these things,' Sergeant Quinn observed. 'I mean, it's not — '

'British? No, that's exactly what I thought. Seems quite appropriate that it's made in France.' Jarrett took his seat and dug his thumbs deep into his waistcoat pockets. It was something he frequently did when he was about to change the subject. 'Tell me about the editor.'

'McGovern? Largely a waste of time, Superintendent. As you suspected, he was more interested in anything Lyle may have written down than in the dead man himself. If he was heartbroken he made a wonderful job of hiding it.'

Jarrett nodded, gave the matter some thought, then just as quickly cast McGovern from his mind and indicated the box. 'I don't suppose that's your lunch.'

'Far from it, sir.' The sergeant placed the box on the desk and laid the lid aside. 'I wouldn't normally trouble you with this sort of stuff, but on this occasion there seems to be a bit of a problem.'

Jarrett lifted one of the photographs, turned it over to check the back, then threw it down.

'What exactly is the difficulty?'

'Well, sir, Detective Constable Williamson took it upon himself to stage a one-man raid on The Sensible Man's Bookshop in Freeman's Walk. In this instance he more than just got away with it. The shop assistant took fright and told him everything.'

'And?'

'The six at the front, sir.'

Jarrett flicked six mounted prints forward and lifted them out as a bunch. He went through them one at a time, then threw them into his drawer and put the lid back on the box.

'How many boxes are there, Sergeant?' he asked.

'Six, sir.'

'Incinerate them all.'

'Don't you want to use them as evidence?'

'Not this time. We won't be pursuing it.'

Tommy Quinn looked surprised, but the decision wasn't up to him so there was nothing more to be said. He pulled a fold of paper from his pocket.

'The name of the shop owner,' he said.

'I already know the name,' Jarrett said. 'Right now I want you to see to the telegraph, then attend to burning the boxes. Do it personally, Sergeant. The men are only human and I don't want these things being circulated in every pub in Glasgow tonight.'

'Leave it to me, sir.' Quinn scooped up the strawboard box and the cane maker's catalogue. 'As soon as I get an answer from Sheffield I'll report back.'

⋆ ⋆ ⋆

A sudden movement by Detective Sergeant Morrison brought Charlie Grant out of his trance and back to the present. They had only been on watch for a couple of hours, it having been decided that Mrs Thorburn would not venture out the previous night and therefore retiring to their respective abodes was in order, but already the boredom of it was taking its toll. Had the lady not emerged from the front door of 55a Woodhill Terrace when she did the detectives would probably have been too far gone to notice.

The blue horse-bus was waiting at the corner of Merchiston Place and Ruthven Street for the ten o'clock departure. Mrs Thorburn paid the conductor and took a front seat downstairs. She was not alone. She would be accompanied every yard of the way and followed whenever she left the vehicle, because sooner or later she would almost certainly contact her brother. But whether she was making for his present hideaway or there was some prearranged meeting place remained to be seen.

It was standard practice for the omnibus to stop whenever a lady wished to get on or off, whereas men tended to alight or depart with the vehicle on the move. Some twenty-five minutes after setting off, it came to a halt outside Wylie & Lochhead's store. Davina Thorburn rose, checked to make sure she had her bits and pieces, and quickly made her way to where the immaculate conductor was proudly making sure that there were no impediments to her reaching the broad pavement. Male barrow-pushers attempting to overtake on the inside were blocked by a stiff arm, small delivery boys trying the same got a clip round the ear.

Within the store, Mrs Thorburn paused briefly in the foyer where she was confronted by a spacious street-level floor and three lofty open galleries. Although the building stretched 200 feet from Buchanan Street to Mitchell Street, an enormous cupola of ground glass covered the entire construction and cast a perfect shadow-free light over every item, however small. According to a sign by the entrance, the proprietors seemed to be particularly proud of their steam-powered lifting device which elevated those ladies and gentlemen to the upper galleries if they found the stairs either tiresome or difficult.

After a few moments, Mrs Thorburn set off along the centre aisle at a brisk rate of knots, weaving in and out of the dithering mass as though aware of being followed. This tactic made it very difficult for Morrison to keep sight of her, so when she turned abruptly right he had to make a snap decision. He turned right too, but in the passage immediately parallel to her, dividing his attention between his target and those whose shuffling and pondering were impeding his progress.

Then, completely unexpectedly, she vanished. This woman of medium height and unremarkable dress had become invisible in a sea of toppers and feathers. Morrison stopped, craned his neck and turned in a full circle, apologizing all the time to those whose progress he was now impeding.

Grant wasn't going to like this. Not one bit.

* * *

A mile or so further on, the gaunt man who had been sitting immediately in front of Mrs Thorburn rose from his seat on the horse-bus and proceeded to the conductor's platform. With that innate ability to calculate possessed by all he stepped from the slowly moving vehicle, paused momentarily to allow a cab to pass, then hurried to the pavement through a narrow gap between the rear of the Hansom and the snorting Clydesdale of a brewer's dray. A few feet behind, Charlie Grant did likewise.

Fifteen years and Grant still recognized him. It wasn't just the stiff ticket-of-leave picture Tommy Quinn had unearthed that triggered his memory. The image had that total lack of personality and character that was the inevitable result of having to hold a pose longer than was either natural or comfortable. It probably had more to do with the fact that it had been Detective Constable Grant's first involvement in a murder case and for that reason was more memorable than those which had occurred since.

Of course the eyes were unmistakable, which was no doubt why the thin man kept his face down and glanced at no one, either when he boarded the bus or left it. Even now, walking at a half-trot across the desolate and brick-strewn wasteland that used to be the absorbed village of Lower Govan, his head was down and his gaze fixed on the uneven and rubbley ground. If he was at all conscious of anyone in pursuit of him he gave no outward indication.

All that remained of Clyde Loan was a single, derelict cottage and the demolishers would soon take care of that. But it served his purpose for the time being. He was a squatter, paying no rent and asking only for a roof over his head and the peace to get on with what he had to do. The few shillings Davina passed to him on the bus got him all the provisions he required. His needs were few.

Even when he reached the old door he failed to look round, but merely pushed it open, disappeared into the gloomy interior and let it swing shut with a clatter. When Charlie Grant let himself in he kept hold of the warped timber until it had settled quietly in the jamb. No sense in advertising his presence any more than was absolutely necessary.

The two downstairs rooms were without doors or windows, but this was not due to any act of vandalism. Instead, the pile of chopped timber and the short-hafted axe at the foot of the narrow, rickety stairs revealed that the hunted man had a wood-burner up there. So he at least had heat and a means of cooking.

Charlie Grant slowly ascended the stairs, but it proved impossible to avoid loose or creaky treads. When he reached the small upper landing Lawrence Short was sitting at the far side of an old table, just staring at him but quite unperturbed.

'Come in, Mr Grant,' he said, entirely without malice. 'Take a seat if you wish. I can't guarantee it won't fall to pieces like everything else in here.'

'You remember me, then,' Charlie said, drawing the chair forward and tentatively sitting on it.

'Yes, I remember you. You stood up for me at the time, but that arrogant bugger Barrowman wouldn't listen to you. It all came back to me when I saw you on the bus.' Short laughed in a low, hoarse way. 'Why were you following me?'

Charlie shrugged.

'Call it preventive policing,' he said. 'The knife-thrower was not a clever move.'

Short was grinning at him now.

'I agree,' he said. 'Very foolish. But you can't really haul me back in on his word alone, can you . . . ?'

'Inspector.'

'Well, can you?' If Short was afraid he made an excellent job of concealing it. He turned in his chair and pushed a smoke-blackened tin pot into the glowing embers that were never allowed to die out completely. 'Tea, Inspector? Won't take a minute. It's been boiled already.'

'Not for me, thanks.'

'As you wish.' Short turned once more in his direction. 'You didn't answer me. Can you send me back there on the strength of his word alone?'

'You are on ticket-of-leave. Police concerns for public safety ought to be enough.' Charlie Grant paused briefly. 'Of course, there's Lyle.'

Short stared at him as though trying to get into his thoughts.

'What about him?'

'So the name does mean something to you.'

'How could it not? Lyle was the cheap scratcher who gave me the name.'

'Was?' Grant jumped on this. 'You know he's dead.'

'I was referring to the trial.'

'Only a handful of people know what happened to Lyle, and one of them is the person who killed him. Tell me what you did, Mr Short.'

Mr Short. It had been a very long time since anyone had called him that, or indeed showed him any respect whatsoever. His eyes glazed over as he leapt back through the years to the moment he was first arrested and all civility ceased.

'You know I didn't kill Mary,' he said quietly.

'Yes, I know.' What mattered now was keeping Short tranquil and, hopefully, co-operative. Grant went on, 'Was it Norman Leckie?'

A thin smile flitted briefly on Short's lips.

'He put me away,' he said. 'When I heard he had died I felt cheated. He was top of my list up till then.'

Inspector Grant endeavoured to stay as nonchalant as possible.

'So you have a list. Who is top now?' But Short would not be drawn. Grant continued, 'You didn't tell me if Leckie killed your wife.'

Short rose slowly from his chair, lifted a dirty rag and used it to remove the pot from the embers. He made a single enamelled mug of tea and returned to his place at the table.

'What difference would it make now?' he asked. 'Leckie's in Hell with the rest of them.'

'Lyle too?'

'Of course Lyle.'

'Anyone else?'

This time Short laughed more heartily than

his usual hoarse bark.

'You are asking me to do your job for you,' he said. 'Why should I?'

'You said it yourself. I stood up for you, but I didn't have the clout to do anything about it.'

Short nodded.

'It wasn't Leckie,' he whispered. 'He wouldn't have the guts. God knows how he ever became foreman.'

Charlie Grant's thoughts were tumbling now. The implication was that only one other person could have removed Mary Short from this world. Then his attention was caught by the actions of the man on the far side of the rough-hewn table, who had abruptly laid down his drinking mug with a clatter and was flexing his fingers.

'Something wrong?' Grant asked.

'Cramp.'

'Try touching something cold. That usually — '

Suddenly, Charlie Grant was on his feet, ready for God knew what. Something unexpected was taking place.

Short's chair clattered on the stone floor and he pushed himself away from the table to stagger towards the open doorway. His world, such as it was, had come unstuck in the last few seconds. It started swaying at the very edge of his vision, and rapidly began to convulse, so quickly that the floor was rising and falling in great waves. He dropped to his knees, but the coarse and twisted timber was closer than he thought and the unexpected jolt surged through him like lightning. Nothing was clear any more; everything was wildly bright and indistinct. A dream image shimmered and danced, and was somehow vaguely human in form. This being was shouting at him from far away, or he may have been whispering inside his head. And the pain was in every part of him now, burning. Then the heat in his guts became excruciating, intolerable, more hideously agonizing than any mortal man should have to endure.

It lasted only a few seconds, but to him it might have been an endless horror.

Then there was nothing at all.

* * *

As soon as Tommy Quinn received a response from Sheffield everything else was put to one side in his haste to inform Superintendent Jarrett.

'Just over two months ago, sir,' he said, placing the cane brochure on the boss's jotter. 'One makila only to Cameron and

Stuart, Gentleman's Accessories, Bath Street. Apparently it was a special order in that it was requested by a customer rather than an item for stock. They can be sure of that because it was urgent and carried a special delivery surcharge.'

'Then let's hope these people in Bath Street can give us something to go on.' Jarrett felt reasonably confident, but at the same time it would be surprising if a professional killer were to give his real name and address. Always assuming he was a professional, of course. 'See to it, Sergeant. Priority.'

'Sir.' Tommy Quinn paused briefly at the door. 'The photographs have gone the way of all things, Superintendent. I attended to it when I was waiting for Sheffield to get back to me.'

'Excellent, Quinn, thank you.'

'Would you like me to take that matter any further?'

'No, I want him to stew in his own juices. The individual concerned now knows that his shop was raided, and unless he is incredibly stupid he also knows that my attention will have been drawn to it.' Jarrett adopted his smug, self-satisfied face and nodded approvingly at his own cleverness. 'I have every intention of allowing him to squirm and cringe on the far side of the dining-room, and may even nod in his direction or give him a little wave. Such men do not deserve a swift fate. I want him to cook low down in the oven for a long time.'

'He might break and run for it, sir.'

'And leave his shop? Not to mention some pretty expensive equipment. No, Sergeant Quinn, this one has varnished himself into a corner and there is nothing he can do but wait.'

Quinn was only minutes out of the office when Charlie Grant arrived. He slumped into a vacant seat and looked for all the world like a runner who had been pipped at the post.

'I need a blood wagon to take Short to the mortuary,' he said flatly. 'He chose to take poison rather than surrender.'

Jarrett stared at him for some time.

'Best way, I suppose,' he said eventually. 'He would only have gone back to the asylum for the rest of his life.'

'An asylum he should never have been in to start with.'

'Sorry?'

'Short didn't kill his wife. I knew that back then but Barrowman wouldn't listen. I suppose when you are young and new to the job you don't want to go up against your superiors.' Grant fell silent for a few moments, then added, 'He spent fifteen years in the madhouse because I wasn't pushy enough, and now he's dead because I was too pushy.'

If the inspector was looking for sympathy he had come to the wrong place. In Henry Jarrett's book the best remedy for self-pity was work.

'So if Short didn't murder his wife,' the superintendent said, 'who did?'

'His sister, Mrs Davina Thorburn.'

'Did he admit that?'

'He didn't have to. It's as plain as the nose on your face that he took the blame on her behalf. She tried to indict the neighbour, Norman Leckie, who seemingly had been dallying with Mary Short, and when that failed Short himself carried the proverbial can for it.'

'Why would he do that?'

'Brotherly love? The jury spared him because of his wife's incessant nagging about money. It was accepted that she had driven him over the edge and into temporary insanity. Mrs Thorburn had no such excuse. She got rid of a woman she felt was making her brother's life a hell, but that alone would not have saved her bacon. They would have hanged her.'

'Did Short confirm her guilt before he died?'

'Not in as many words, but it is clear what happened. Davina Thorburn drowned Mary Short.'

'And got away with it.'

'Got away with murder, yes, but not necessarily attempted murder.'

Jarrett looked quizzically at the inspector.

'I'm afraid that's a shade too deep for me, Charlie,' he admitted.

'Well, let me put it this way,' Grant said, in a conspiratorial voice, 'I expect to see the last act of this small drama being carried out in the very near future.'

Then Tommy Quinn returned from a trip to Bath Street and a perusal of the order books of Cameron and Stuart, Gentleman's Accessories.

'According to the manager the makila was bought by James Miller, 14 Hillpark Gardens,' he offered reservedly.

'Permit me to venture a guess,' Jarrett said. 'Hillpark Gardens exists, but there is no 14 and no James Miller.'

'Afraid not, sir.'

'I didn't think there would be. Not for a single moment.'

11

When Henry Jarrett arrived at the superior guesthouse in time for dinner, Elsie Maitland was delighted to see him but Edgar Trimmer was not. Inwardly, the bookseller was a churning mass of anger and fear because his shop had been invaded and valuable items of gentleman's art removed, yet he had not been charged by the upstart detective who had taken it upon himself to adopt the moral high ground and decide what was right and what was not. Now Jarrett, who could not possibly be in ignorance of the events in Freeman's Walk, was nodding sociably to him and the others as though absolutely nothing had happened.

Even the attractive Mrs Maitland still smiled at him, suggesting that Jarrett had not confided in her. But he would, of course. That was inevitable, because Lizzie Gill was her maid, and because they were as close as peas in a pod, Jarrett and the lady of the house. This latter fact further fuelled Trimmer's loathing for the superintendent, who, it was generally believed by all in the dining-room, was regularly and vigorously depriving the widow of her pantaloons and casting them aside. Students of such things had pointed out that no corsets ever graced Mrs Maitland's drying line. She fed her husband to death while scrupulously preserving her own girlish form, inherited a nice property and an undisclosed sum, and was now quite clearly on the verge of frittering all that on a colonial copper whose sole purpose in life was to bring misery to those who did not meet his exacting standards. Without quite realizing it, Trimmer's fish knife turned in his fingers until he was gripping its handle like a dagger.

But instead of jumping to his feet and launching a frontal attack on his sworn enemy, he merely nodded back and retreated behind his evening paper.

After dinner, Jarrett retired to his room, where he positioned himself in front of his fern case and waited for Elsie Maitland to arrive. She would not be long, of course, because he had made it clear from his expression that all was not well and that they had to talk.

Within minutes, the lady gently rapped the door, entered without bidding and closed it softly behind her.

'What's wrong?' she whispered, concerned.

Under normal circumstances Jarrett would

never have shown photographs of such a nature to a lady, but Mrs Maitland had been married, was concerned with the girl's depressed state and, perhaps most important of all, to describe the items would be even more tasteless and difficult. He placed the pile of half-plate prints face down on his small side-table and indicated them with a slight jerk of the head.

The lady impassively considered each picture, then returned them to the table and stood, hands clasped, waiting.

'Trimmer,' Henry Jarrett said softly. 'One of Tommy Quinn's men raided his shop. It was all entirely fortuitous, if that is the right word.'

Elsie Maitland's expression never changed.

'He leaves,' she said. 'Now.'

'No.' Jarrett briefly placed a hand on her clasped fingers as he rose from his chair and told her with his eyes that this was not how he wanted it. When he spoke it was barely more audible than a breath. 'Trimmer must not be allowed to walk away from his crimes so easily. I was interested to note that you said 'he leaves' not 'they leave'. You knew instinctively that the blame was all on one side and that the girl would not willingly have taken part in such a thing, whether for money or any other reason. That's why I want her story. I suspect it may have been worse than the improper use of a camera.'

'In that case I don't think she'll talk to you, not about that sort of thing.'

'You, then. Would she talk to you?'

'Up to a point, perhaps, but if she thinks she will have to stand in the witness box in front of a courtful of men, I'm afraid — '

'She won't, I promise you. There is no question of that happening. She would come out of it in a worse state than Trimmer, so I wouldn't put her through it.' Jarrett gave her a reassuring smile and placed a hand on her shoulder. 'Neither this address nor the girl's reputation will be compromised for a worthless creature like that.'

'Are you telling me that the price of maintaining her name is to allow him to escape?'

'Prison, yes, but not the sort of justice he fears most — ruination. If we took him to court he would be fined five pounds as a first-time offender, and that's it. There would be no possibility of proving that a crime had been committed against the person of the girl and her word would not be accepted by a jury that would probably view her as fair game. That's why it has to be settled here, using fear as a weapon in the same way that he must have used it against her.'

Mrs Maitland nodded appreciatively.

'I'll talk to her,' she said softly. 'One way or another I'll get the story.'

'But don't warn Trimmer off until I am ready. Be as civil to him as you can manage and tell Lizzie to continue to serve him in the dining-room, but make it clear that she does not have to have any other dealings with him. Now that you know she has a problem with that man and are not holding her responsible for anything he has no hold over her.'

Suddenly, Jarrett fell silent and Mrs Maitland moved towards the door because Lizzie was coming up the stairs, calling for her. The lady of the house then disappeared, but only briefly. When she returned she wore that apologetic look the superintendent had come to expect when his peace was about to be shattered.

'I hate to tell you this, Henry,' Mrs Maitland whispered, 'but . . . '

'There's a young constable waiting for me in the drawing-room.'

'Not exactly. Lizzie put him in the kitchen.'

* * *

Perhaps in years to come, when Constable Archie MacLean achieved some exalted position in the City of Glasgow Police, he would look back over his time in the force to the days when he thought he was destined always to be the one who was sent to fetch the superintendent from his nice warm digs.

'The Khyber Pass, sir,' he said solemnly. 'Inspector Grant and Sergeant Quinn are at the scene.'

'And the chief constable?'

'I believe he's at a dinner in the City Chambers, Superintendent. I don't think he has been informed.'

The narrow defile to the west of the Botanic Gardens, popularly known as the Khyber Pass, was popular with lovers for obvious reasons. But not on this occasion. It was just 8.00 p.m. Already uniformed officers were turning them away and advising them to find another, equally suitable spot for whatever they had in mind.

Jarrett stepped down from the cab and raised a quizzical eyebrow at the sight of Charlie Grant's broad grin.

'It always happens sooner or later, Superintendent,' the Inspector said chirpily. 'They always make a mistake, and this time it was a big one.'

Jarrett looked down at the dead face, with its neatly trimmed moustache and receding hair that made him look ten years older than he probably was, then let his eyes travel downwards to the shiny boots. There was something very military about the man, and he could readily imagine him stepping out boldly in life.

'Constable Gutteridge saw the actual attack,' Grant continued. 'He was no more than thirty feet away and witnessed everything. The assailant came out of the shadows, inflicted a single jab to the heart, then saw Gutteridge and showed him a clean pair of heels.'

'So . . . ?'

'Exactly, sir. No time to go through the pockets. This time we've got it all.'

Tommy Quinn had been kneeling beside the corpse, but now he rose and held out both hands so that Jarrett could see the haul.

'Watch with inscription, gold signet ring, notebook, a few coins, door key and a monogrammed handkerchief.' Quinn, like Grant, was evidently pleased. 'Oh, I almost forgot, Superintendent. He has an Adams revolver in his coat pocket.'

'A what?'

'An Adams revolver, sir. Loaded but unfired.'

'And you almost forgot? How many guns have you encountered in your brief but illustrious career, Sergeant?'

'Very few, sir.'

‘How many?’

‘None.’

‘Then I should have thought that it might make an impression on you. Show it to me.’

Quinn handed the various bit and pieces to Gutteridge who was hovering nearby in anticipation of Jarrett’s questions, then bobbed back down again and retrieved the heavy handgun.

‘If it was meant to be for protection it wasn’t much use, sir, was it?’ he said brightly, then reverted to regulation deadpan when Jarrett failed to be amused.

The superintendent examined the piece briefly then dropped it into his own capacious pocket. He took the notebook from Gutteridge’s miscellaneous collection and flicked through the pages.

‘Perhaps an address,’ he said, more to himself than the rest.

‘With respect, sir,’ Charlie Grant observed, ‘you don’t write down your own name and address unless you happen to have the memory of a flea.’

‘Any address, Inspector,’ Jarrett replied, perhaps too sharply. Grant was only trying to be helpful. ‘Something that will bounce straight back to him.’

Then, quite unexpectedly, the night produced its best bit of luck in the form of a small receipt, folded twice and tucked into the notebook.

'Now, that's what I call landing on your feet,' Charlie Grant said. 'That'll be our gentleman there, all right.'

'Thaddeus Lorimer, 56 Drewitt's Lane.' Somehow, Jarrett thought, it was more than likely genuine. 'Any idea where that is, Constable?'

'Just on the other side of the boilermaker's works, sir,' Gutteridge said quickly, ever anxious to please. 'Start of my beat.'

'Good man.' Jarrett considered the young officer for a few moments. Just like MacLean, bright and eager. 'How did you happen to come across the event without the attacker seeing you coming.'

'Well, sir,' Gutteridge admitted, 'just as I came round the corner I saw this gent approaching. All of a sudden the killer came out of nowhere, stabbed him, then immediately shot the crow at the first peep of the whistle.'

'Could you identify him?'

'Afraid not, sir. He was about the same height as this one and generally the same build, but it was too far away and it's always a bit on the dark side in the Khyber Pass.'

⋆ ⋆ ⋆

56 Drewitt's Lane existed all right, but this was no lodging house and there was no one at home. But that was more or less what Jarrett expected, given the presence of a key among Lorimer's possessions. He pushed open the door and led the way into a small hallway. The house, small and narrow, consisted of one room off to the right and steep stairs immediately ahead, which no doubt led up to the one and only bedroom. Still, the place was neat in a sparse way, which again suggested a military sort with few portable possessions.

'You take this room, Sergeant,' he said. 'Inspector, come with me.'

As expected, the small bedroom contained only what was required and no more. There was a neat, well-made bed, a small trunk and an oil lamp. Lorimer may have been part of the same group as Hartman and Fenton, but he was an entirely different fish.

Charlie Grant took a quick look beneath the thin mattress and found nothing, while Jarrett lifted the lid of the cabin box and surveyed its contents. This was not difficult to do. Apart from three neatly folded shirts, spare socks and johns, and a spare pair of trousers which matched the suit he was found in, the only items of interest were a small leather Bible and a large notepad.

'A great one for keeping notes, our Mr Lorimer,' the superintendent observed. 'What do you make of this?'

Inspector Grant slowly turned over the pages, but it was clear from the outset that it might as well have been Swahili for all the sense it made.

'Code?' he half-stated.

'Yes, but why?'

'Maybe we'll know that when we've broken it.'

'That won't be a problem.' Jarrett retrieved the book and smiled thinly. 'Tommy Quinn can take care of that.'

'He understands these things?'

'Not yet, but he will.'

Downstairs, Sergeant Quinn was raking a poker through the ashes in the old black Albert Kitchener range when his superiors joined him.

'Cold as a — '

'Whore's heart,' Grant offered.

Quinn gave him a disapproving look.

'Not been any cooking done on this for a long time,' he informed them. He jerked the poker in the direction of a large tin scuttle. 'No coal and no kindling, either, so he hasn't even been heating the place.'

'No need at this time of the year,' Jarrett said. 'He probably ate at a pub or a barrow.

This place was only somewhere to put his head down.'

'Or lie low,' Grant suggested.

'Excuse me!' the exclamation came from a man at least a foot smaller than his voice. 'May I ask who you are?'

Despite his diminutive stature, the little man had all the guts in the world. They could have been robbers, these three, or worse, yet he didn't retreat from the open doorway when Charlie Grant approached.

'Police,' the inspector said and showed him his badge. 'And you?'

'Walter Moore. I own this property.' He looked beyond Grant at Henry Jarrett, correctly identifying him as the superior officer. 'Where is Mr Lorimer?'

Inspector Grant ignored this. Detectives ask questions; they don't answer them.

'Can you confirm that Thaddeus Lorimer was your tenant?'

'Yes, he took the house for three months with an option to renew the agreement. I was coming to see him today about that.'

'So when did you last see him?' he demanded.

Moore was concerned and showed it.

'Has something — ?'

'Just answer the question. When did you last see him?'

'I saw him on the passing a few times, but I haven't actually spoken to him for some weeks. He would pay a month in advance, you see.'

'You didn't see him today?'

'No.'

'Did you see anyone else near this property, perhaps loitering in the area?'

'No, no one.' Moore's patience with the officers was fast running out and it was clear that he was not the sort of man who was easily brow-beaten. He had obviously never been in trouble with the law. 'Don't you think you should tell me exactly what is going on? If my tenant is in trouble — '

'Thaddeus Lorimer is dead,' Superintendent Jarrett stated flatly, giving it a few seconds to sink in. 'He was murdered.'

The news stunned Moore and caused him to raise a hand to his brow in a most dramatic fashion.

'Murdered?' he breathed. 'Mr Lorimer. Surely not.'

'I'm afraid so. Now perhaps you understand how important it is for you to help us with our enquiries.'

'Of course . . . '

'Superintendent Jarrett.'

'Superintendent. I would be glad to help you in any way I can, but I don't know very much. Nothing at all, really.'

'In my experience that isn't usually the case,' Jarrett said. 'Tell me what you know about the deceased.'

'Well, he was a Canadian gentleman. Very well-mannered and entirely sober in his ways.'

'Church-going? I noticed a Bible upstairs.'

'Yes, I believe he was. Now that I come to think of it, yes, he did set off every Sunday morning with the Good Book under his arm. It occurred to me that he was putting most of the locals to shame.'

'Do you know which church he attended?'

'I assume it was the Church of Scotland in Albert Avenue, judging by how long it took him to get there and back.'

Jarrett smiled as it occurred to him that Mr Moore was more of an observer than he liked to make out, or even cared to admit to himself. It was a sovereign to a penny that not much went by him unseen.

'Very helpful, Mr Moore, thank you. Now, do you know where Mr Lorimer ate? He didn't do any cooking here.'

'Probably the Park restaurant. It's a good, clean place which would suit a man like Mr Lorimer extremely well. It's just round the corner by the fountain.'

'One last thing, sir. Do you know what Mr Lorimer did for a living?'

'Why, nothing. I believe he was visiting the city and was intending to return home to Canada in the near future. Since he had no clear plans he took the place for three months in the first instance. That, I think, is about all I can tell you.'

* * *

Since it was in no one's interest to spin this day out any longer than was absolutely necessary, and Henry Jarrett in particular had no wish to stretch the admirable Mrs Maitland's patience to breaking point, he made for the City Mortuary in the hope that Dr Hamilton had completed his initial examination of Lorimer's body. Charlie Grant, in turn, went off to shake up the minister of the Albert Avenue church in his manse, while Tommy Quinn pursued whatever leads might be found in the Park Restaurant.

The wound on Lorimer's chest matched the others exactly, only this time Jarrett was able to supply the necessary information regarding the type of weapon that had been used. As far as the clothes were concerned, everything had been purchased locally and nothing had been mended or darned. This merely reinforced Jarrett's view of Lorimer as being more fastidious than the others and perhaps from a different background. Beyond that, little emerged from Dr Hamilton's initial inspection of the corpse and it was unlikely that anything would.

All three reached Jarrett's office around the same time with little to show for their efforts other than that which could have been deduced without the loss of shoe leather. But at least it confirmed that Lorimer, Hartman and Fenton used both the church and the restaurant as their meeting places — and no doubt other sites as well which were more convenient for Hartman and Fenton — suggesting that they had a policy of not being seen together. But that had already been shown by Hartman's displeasure at Lorimer's visit to Sweeney's house in Rowan Way.

What it did not do was provide the slightest clue as to what exactly they were up to. That information was still as elusive as it had been on day one.

* * *

Miss Ada Findlay was ageless and, to all except Jake McGovern, the *Advertiser*'s editor, quite terrifying. He alone received courtesy and a smile, while all the rest had to make do with a glare like cold steel. It was said that she had been left over from the previous administration and that no one had the nerve to ask her what she did. In fact, she was McGovern's safety net. No one got past her without a damned good reason. But for her he would have been horse-whipped a dozen times or more.

'Just arrived by messenger, Mr McGovern,' she said brightly, placing the parcel before him. 'It would appear that you have an admirer.'

McGovern tugged open the string bow and laid back the heavy brown paper. It was a large seed cake with a brand new knife wrapped in oil paper and pressed into it.

'Very nice, Miss Findlay,' he said warmly. 'Care for a slice?'

'I think not, sir, if you don't mind.'

'Nor I.' McGovern sat back in his chair and nodded admiringly at the gift. 'Telegraph Central Headquarters and let Inspector Grant know he was absolutely right.'

12

At precisely eight o'clock the following morning, Henry Jarrett hung his coat on the stag horn rack, placed Lorimer's large notebook squarely on his large jotter and took his seat behind the desk. After a few moments in which to correlate his thoughts he pressed one of the two large brass buttons on his new electric 'requestor', as he fondly termed it. This one would bring Sergeant Quinn hurrying to the main office. Inspector Grant was otherwise employed.

When Jarrett returned to 76 Delmont Avenue the previous evening, he had found a very angry Elsie Maitland just managing to control her desire to turf Edgar Trimmer out on his ear. At first, and as expected, Lizzie had refused to say what had occurred between Trimmer and herself, but Mrs Maitland was nothing if not persistent and before long she had the whole story. Henry Jarrett arrived just as she was making her way up the stairs for a final showdown. With no little difficulty he managed to persuade her yet again to reveal nothing and treat Trimmer as though everything was rosy in the garden.

Evicting the man would not solve anything.

Tommy Quinn chapped the door, then swiftly entered the office without waiting for an invitation.

'Sir,' he said, but his cheery expression was tinged ever so slightly with apprehension.

Jarrett pushed the notebook in his direction.

'Do you know what this is?' he asked.

Quinn lifted the book, flicked through the pages, then tucked it under his arm.

'Presumably you want me to find out about the code, Superintendent,' he speculated.

'No, Sergeant, I don't. I already know what it is.'

'Then . . . ?'

'It's called the Shelton Code. I was pretty sure of it when I first saw it, but I wanted to verify it before committing myself. Basically, it isn't a code at all, but a system of short writing used by Samuel Pepys and Sir Isaac Newton to allow them to write quickly and probably protect their work from prying eyes. A consonant is printed as is, or represented by a symbol if you want to be really careful, while the five vowels are just dots in a semi-circle to the right of it, with A at the top and U at the bottom. So a C with a T above it and a dot between would be CAT, while a C with a T below it and a dot between is CUT.

You would be surprised at how fast you can learn to use this system.'

Quinn grimaced. The uneasiness he had felt all the way along the corridor had not been misplaced.

'I suppose you would like me to decode the notebook, Superintendent,' he said.

'No one better for the task, Sergeant. Quick as you like, if you don't mind. Lorimer didn't protect his information just for fun.'

* * *

It was just about then that Charlie Grant, with a uniformed constable in tow, arrived at 55a Woodhill Terrace, pulled the bell chain until it was plain that no one was going to answer, then decided to investigate the rear of the property, just in case access proved easier there. The small rear door was closed but not locked, as though Mrs Thorburn had anticipated just such a visit.

'Mrs Thorburn!' The inspector moved cautiously through the long kitchen and into the narrow, oak-panelled hallway. 'Are you in, Mrs Thorburn?'

He paused on the third step of the staircase with his left hand on the polished rail. At this point he was ready for anything, because it was now clear that Davina Thorburn was capable of just that. It was certainly not beyond the realm of possibility that she might be waiting up there in the shadows, determined not to go alone but to take her tormentor to Hell with her. Charlie Grant had been aware of a certain abnormal streak in her character, perhaps even the kind of self-deluding madness that would lead her to try to kill a man by sending him a poisoned cake. Perhaps it was brain fever stemming from a fixation with her brother and his fate that went beyond what was natural.

Indeed, a suggestion of the unnatural occurred at Short's trial but was not pursued, perhaps because it was too indelicate. Yet it could explain much. The idea of Mrs Thorburn killing Mary Short to stop her nagging her beloved brother seemed just a little far fetched, but green-eyed jealousy finally reaching boiling point was quite another matter. Charlie Grant could understand that. So much so, in fact, that it might be interesting, if ultimately pointless, to find out when Mr Thorburn died, and how.

He continued up the stairs to the half-landing, paused briefly, then made the tight turn and progressed to the square upper hall. He then turned the large handle on the closest bedroom door and pushed it open. The room was empty. He crossed to the one facing it and did the same. This door swung back to reveal Davina Thorburn lying on the bed, fully clothed in her Sundays and with her hands clasped on her lower ribs. She was never colourful at the best of times, but now she was a mealy parchment shade and her lips were grey.

When Charlie Grant placed his knuckles on her forehead she was ice cold.

'I want you to stay here until the medical officer arrives, just to make sure no one rifles the place,' he said to the young constable. 'Make yourself a cup of tea, son, but I'd think twice before eating anything if I were you.'

* * *

A summons to appear in Rattray's plush office was never welcome at the best of times, but when it was half-expected and the reason for it self-evident, Henry Jarrett decided to get it over with there and then. The temptation to postpone it was strong, but the desire to find out who had been complaining to Rattray this time was even stronger.

In the event, no one was specifically named. Rattray gestured carelessly towards the empty chair and offered Jarrett a cheroot from his silver box. It was declined.

'Forgot,' he said loudly. 'Don't smoke,

don't drink, don't gamble. Can't be seduced or frightened off by threats. You had quite a reputation in Hong Kong, Superintendent.'

'If you have a weakness they will find it,' Jarrett replied. 'It's how the gangs work; it's how they control people.'

'But they didn't get to you, eh? Very admirable, Jarrett, very admirable.' The CC applied a lucifer to his cigar and gave it a good draw or two before continuing. 'You're not a brother. That could be restricting, you know. If you ever want to occupy this seat you would be well advised to consider it.'

'I'm not a joiner, Chief Constable,' Jarrett admitted. 'Sorry.'

'Oh, it's no skin off my nose, I can assure you. It's just that it would make it easier for me to say what I have to say.'

'And that is?'

'The Canadian business. Time to draw a line under it, Jarrett. As a gesture of goodwill to our Canadian cousins the Chamber of Commerce is providing suitable burial plots in the Necropolis, so there will be no paupers' graves for these men. Can't do better than that, can we?'

Jarrett felt, and looked, confused.

'But — '

'No buts, Superintendent, the matter is at an end. Trust me when I tell you that this affair goes beyond the law.'

'With respect, Chief Constable, nothing is beyond the law.'

Rattray was in no mood for arguing, but somehow managed to keep an even tone and an impassive expression. But how long he could hold this remained to be seen.

'There are certain things which may be deemed above and beyond common law,' he said. 'The security of the nation, for example, or the welfare of the monarchy.'

'Are you telling me — ?'

'I'm telling you that the investigation is over, closed, finished. The alternative is that both of our careers are in jeopardy. I don't think I can put it more strongly than that.'

'No, I don't think you can, sir.' Jarrett chose to get quickly to his feet rather than be dismissed by someone he had little or no respect for. Yet, for all his dislike of the man, he couldn't help feeling slightly sorry for him. Rattray was afraid, not for his physical wellbeing, but rather for his standing in the community. Such things were of paramount importance to such a man. 'I'll do as you say. The Canadian file will be closed.'

Rattray nodded, but said nothing. He merely rose from his seat and stood at the large window, hands behind his back, indicating that the meeting was at an end and he had won.

* * *

Within the hour, Charlie Grant was firmly ensconced in his favourite chair in the superintendent's office, his notebook open on the desk for Jarrett to see the final curtain. After his chief had related Rattray's instructions, he said, 'Can I take your promise at face value, Superintendent?'

'You can indeed, Inspector. The Canadian file will be closed.'

'When you have the killer.'

'I didn't say that to the CC.' There was a wicked twinkle in Jarrett's eyes as he turned Grant's open notebook around and quickly flicked through the pages. 'At least this business is over and done with. Best way, I think.'

'Best way by far. It would have been impossible at this late stage to prove that she murdered Mary Short, and as for the attempted murder of Jake McGovern . . . well, I don't think we could have made that one stick. The delivery company said that the cake had been handed in by a veiled woman, so identification was not on the cards. Even through I saw Short passing a small parcel to her on the omnibus I didn't know at the time what it could be. To be honest, it wasn't until after Short had killed himself that I guessed what she was about to do. The irony of it is that she died not knowing we couldn't prove anything.'

'Perhaps it wasn't a consideration. She had no one left on this side of the Great Divide now, so it may be that she chose to cross over. She might not even have given us a further thought, Inspector, however bruising that might be for our collective self-respect.'

Charlie Grant smiled as he retrieved his book. This case at least was closed.

* * *

It was in the early afternoon that Tommy Quinn finally emerged from the tiny cubicle at the end of the corridor that he called his office. The end of the Canadian problem was now in plain sight.

Charlie Grant, now fully back on the case and eager to put CC Rattray's nose out of joint, sat at one end of Jarrett's desk and waited for some sign from above.

'Good stuff, is it, Sergeant?' Henry Jarrett asked.

'It's all here, sir.' Quinn laid down Lorimer's large notebook and referred instead to his own transcript. 'First, it isn't a diary, it's a log. He was recording everything that transpired for his superiors back home. Which brings me to a very important point. Hartman, Fenton and Lorimer were not Canadians. It would appear from the instructions they were given at the start of their mission that it is standard practice for Union agents to pass themselves off as Canadians in foreign ports to avoid violating neutrality arrangements.'

'Union?' Jarrett interrupted, glancing at Charlie Grant. 'Are you telling me that this is some kind of extension of the American War?'

'That's exactly what it is, Superintendent. 'They were ordered to identify, locate and kill a top agent of the CSN, known only as the Ghost by the Pinkerton Agency. The CSN is the Confederate States Navy, sir.'

'Why here?'

'That is the very point. The Clyde shipyards have supplied numerous blockade runners to the Confederates, much to the annoyance of the Northerners. The one they call the Ghost is over here buying for the CSN and they were out to stop him, but not only did they fail to achieve any of their three aims, it would appear that he is considerably more skilled in the art of killing than they were.' Sergeant Quinn paused, but briefly. 'After Fenton was slain, Lorimer expressed doubt in the log as to his ability to kill the Ghost. Hartman had been appointed leader of the group, much to Lorimer's disgust since he was an officer and the others were just spies in his opinion. He was also annoyed by the fact that Fenton assumed the role of observer when he, Lorimer, should have been the one watching the progress of the ships. After all, Fenton was there to do the shooting, while Lorimer was the naval expert responsible for locating the vessels the Ghost was after. He felt that it was a typical military mess, where the wrong people are assigned the wrong roles. But most of all he notes his anger at the delay in their wages coming across. Out of sight out of mind, he says. It seems that quite a lot of things annoyed Thaddeus Lorimer.

'Anyway, once Hartman and Fenton were dead there was no one left but him, so he had to retrieve Fenton's Adams revolver from Mrs MacNiven's lodging house and almost scared the poor lady half to death. As we saw it didn't do him much good. It was still in his coat pocket when he was stabbed.

'Incidentally,' Quinn went on, '*Lady Dawn*, *Slanaighear* and *Isle of Mull* are iron-hulled steamboats, currently under construction at Tod and MacGregor's yard.'

'But we checked with Lloyd's,' Charlie Grant objected.

'Yes, but they wouldn't be registered until they had completed their sea trials.'

'Hell!' Grant fell silent for a few moments, then, 'Just out of interest, Sergeant, which of the high points did Fenton use to watch the shipyard.'

'All of them.' Tommy Quinn grinned sheepishly. 'Each one of us could see Tod and MacGregor's yard when we were out that day. It was one feature we all had in common.'

Under different circumstances Henry Jarrett might have found that amusing, but the time factor was preying on his mind and there was no room in his tight, self-imposed schedule for jollification.

'To the point, Sergeant Quinn,' he said. 'Did Lorimer know where the Ghost could be located?'

'No, sir. Truth is, they didn't even know what he looked like. In the log Lorimer clearly states that they must have been compromised, and somehow the Confederacy found out enough about their mission to warn the Ghost that they were out to kill him.'

Jarrett nodded thoughtfully.

'Anything else, Sergeant?'

'Not immediately relevant, sir. There is a list of expenses, including rent, food and several clothing purchases, and a complaint that not a cent had so far been received, but that's it.'

'Fine.' The superintendent fetched his coat from the horn rack. 'If you are quite finished leaving a trail of corpses behind you, Inspector, you might like to accompany me to Tod and MacGregor's shipyard. As for you, Sergeant, I'd like you to call once more on Cameron and Stuart in Bath Street. The address of the buyer of the makila is false, I know, but you might just jog someone's memory. Be a little bit more insistent this time. Scare somebody.'

* * *

The large gates of the shipyard slid open sufficiently to permit the Kinross wagon to enter the cobblestoned forecourt, but the welcome was far from warm. Employment was secure and bonuses were being earned, and anyone who threatened that in any way was no friend of the workforce. The police were never the bearers of good news, especially when they represent the Detective Department.

Henry Jarrett and Charlie Grant stepped down from the wagon and left the uniformed driver to glare silently at the miserable gatekeeper while they headed for the iron stairs that led up to the elevated offices. But they were spared the climb by a well-dressed man who paused briefly on the upper landing then hurried down quickly to meet them.

'I'm afraid both Mr Tod and Mr MacGregor have gone to the Great Majority in recent years,' he said in answer to Jarrett's request for his name. 'The company is now owned by their families. I'm Jack Lowrie, the yard manager.'

'And managing very well by the looks of things,' Grant put in.

'That, sir, is the power of publicity. The whole world knows the name of David Livingstone, the missionary and explorer. Mr Livingstone has a great deal of influence, and I am delighted to say that we were given the order to build the *Lady Nyassa*, a twin-screw steamship, which we shipped out to Africa in sections. That is something he could not have arranged before he became famous.'

'Very impressive,' said the superintendent, 'But I think it best that we get straight to the point, Mr Lowrie. I understand that you now have three vessels under construction for the navy of the Southern States of America.'

Lowrie stared at Jarrett, then at Grant, and for a few moments was at a loss for words. But he wasn't the manager for nothing and soon regained the power of speech.

'We are building three ships for a company in the Azores,' he admitted. 'They are all schooner-rigged, iron-hulled, paddle-steamers with double stacks. I can give you a guided tour if you like.'

'No need. Whether they are destined for the Azores or not is entirely irrelevant. Their ultimate destination is the Confederate States Navy.'

'I can assure you, sir, that Tod and MacGregor have never become embroiled in foreign wars — '

'Please, Mr Lowrie, don't insult me. I didn't come here without first making enquiries. The *Giraffe* was built right here not one year ago. Officially, she was intended as a Glasgow to Belfast packet, but she is currently outrunning Union ships off the east coast of America under her new name of the *Robert E. Lee*.'

Yet again, Lowrie fell momentarily silent. When he finally spoke the friendly tone had gone and he was decidedly hostile.

'Let me tell you a couple of things, Superintendent. First, we do not directly supply vessels to the Confederacy or any other warring nation, but even if we did it is not illegal. The second thing is this: most Glasgow merchants have a vested interest in the South. It's where their cotton and tobacco comes from. Now, I don't know whether you are on some moral crusade, but by picking on me you are in danger of bringing down upon your head the wrath of a lot of very powerful people.'

'Can I take that as a threat made in the presence of Inspector Grant?'

'No threat, Superintendent. I think you already know you've stepped out of line and don't need me to tell you.'

'Perhaps, but this is no moral crusade, Mr Lowrie. We are investigating three murders which we believe are in some way connected to this yard. You would do well to remember that we represent the law of the land.'

It was as though the stuffing had suddenly been knocked out of Lowrie. The pushiness vanished instantly.

'Murder?' he said softly. 'But how?'

'I can't go into that right now. Suffice to say that these ships have so far cost at least three lives and it may not be over yet. If I were you, Mr Lowrie, I would assist the police in every way possible.'

'Yes, of course. But you must realize that I am only the yard manager. I do exactly as I am told.'

'By the families?'

'Not really. They tend to stay out of it. The board, on the other hand, have very fixed objectives.'

'Such as a triumphant Confederacy.'

Lowrie nodded.

'It would seem so,' he said.

'Well, since that does not appear to be likely as things stand perhaps you should consider your own future. If the war ended now what would happen to the shipyard?'

'It would be finished. There's too much wrapped up in those ships. More than a hundred thousand pounds, in fact.'

'And you, of course, would never get another managerial position in any Clyde shipyard,' Charlie Grant said. 'Not with a record like that, Mr Lowrie.'

'The best thing you could do, Mr Lowrie,' Henry Jarrett added quickly, 'is swiftly remember all the things you had decided to conveniently forget.'

* * *

Some days produce the goods. Others are barren and a waste of time from morn to night. This was a good one. Jarrett and Grant weren't the only ones to strike gold.

'Good advice,' Tommy Quinn offered cheerfully when they returned to the office. 'Scaring somebody, I mean. You would be surprised what it can do for the memory.'

'We just found out for ourselves,' Charlie Grant said, reaching for the chair to take the weight off his feet, 'but we'll have your news first.'

'Delighted, Inspector. Well, after reflecting on the matter the senior salesman remembered one vital detail that could lead us to the killer. The shop had merely asked for a name and address as a matter of course, but since they weren't delivering the item it was never found to be false. Anyway, when the customer collected the object he was seen to get into a brougham which the staff recognized as belonging to a regular customer.'

'They must have known this when you first called on them.'

'Of course they did, but no one in the place was going to willingly volunteer information like that. Once they realized that the makila may have been used as a murder weapon it was an entirely different matter.'

'Yes, it always is,' Jarrett said. 'What about the brougham?'

'Owned by Sir Isaac Strickland.'

Charlie Grant sat forward instantly.

'The mill owner?'

'Exactly, Inspector.' Tommy Quinn grimaced and looked decidedly sheepish. 'Unless I'm the world's worst judge of people, one of them will have been in touch with him by now to tell him of our interest.

There was nothing I could do to prevent that.'

'Perhaps it is all for the good.' Jarrett leaned back in his chair and let his thoughts tumble. Then he settled on Trimmer. If things went badly wrong he, Jarrett, might not hold down this position come the morrow, so the fate of the twisted photographer would have to be settled tonight. He had wanted him to squirm a little longer, but that was a risk the superintendent could no longer take if there was any chance of Trimmer escaping unpunished. 'If you were Sir Isaac Strickland, what would you do now?'

Tommy Quinn shrugged.

'Bluff it out? Get in touch with the powers-that-be and try to put a lid on the Detective Department's activities?'

'Possibly, but he has no way of knowing just how much we have found out. These people are only loyal to each other up to a point. If Strickland thought for a moment that he was going to be involved in a common murder investigation he would look out for himself.'

'He is going to get in touch with you,' Charlie Grant said flatly. It wasn't a question, more a statement of fact. 'Look to the third post, Superintendent.'

Henry Jarrett produced his silver hunter

and flicked it open.

'Let's do that,' he said. 'I have already been threatened with early retirement, so what have I got to lose? Within the next half-hour we should know one way or the other.'

13

It came with the third post, a small blue envelope with an entwined IS neatly impressed into the red wax seal. Significantly, it was addressed to the Chief of Detectives and not Chief Constable Rattray. Sir Isaac Strickland was evidently attempting to parley, not bully.

Henry Jarrett flicked open the fresh wax with the tip of his paper knife and withdrew a single fold of matching writing paper. It was brief and to the point — an invitation to the Cressfield Estate in order that both parties might exchange vital information.

'At long and miserable last, gentlemen,' Jarrett said, tucking the envelope and its contents into his inside coat pocket, 'we may have a breakthrough. It is pretty obvious what Strickland is after and I have no doubt he knows what I want.'

On this occasion, and mainly because a deputation would not be conducive to frank discussion, Jarrett decided to go alone. Since neither Grant nor Quinn had anything pressing to hand, they cut the day short and headed for their respective beds. But this was on the understanding that there might be a call-out at any time of the day or night. Judging by recent activity, that was not exactly unlikely.

The butler evidently had orders to admit Jarrett, though under normal circumstances he would have had to judge for himself whether it was the main door or the tradesman's entrance. It was all a question of status and position, and detective superintendent was definitely a borderline ranking.

'Might I ask you to instruct your driver to take that vehicle around to the stable yard,' the butler said. 'It is scarcely a society carriage, sir. Altogether too functional to occupy the forecourt.'

'I'll do that,' Jarrett agreed, 'if you arrange for him to have a cup of tea in the kitchen. I always think you should look after your serfs and minions, don't you?'

The butler's expression remained fixed and unrevealing, but his cold eyes betrayed his inner feelings. This police person was obviously one of those Socialist types who threatened his cherished world of privilege and quality.

'My master is waiting in the drawing-room,' he confided, as though it was a state secret. 'This way, please.'

Sir Isaac Strickland had not quite gone to seed, but it was nevertheless true to say that he enjoyed his grub and no doubt whatever he washed it down with.

'I am not in the habit of beating about the bush, Superintendent Jarrett,' he said, 'so I would like to get straight to the chase, hopefully to our mutual satisfaction.'

'If it isn't, Sir Isaac, there won't be a conclusion.'

Strickland glared at him, but conceded the point and nodded his assent.

'I am told you are in possession of a certain list, sir. Before we go any further you might care to do me the courtesy of confirming or denying this.'

'I have a list of names compiled by the reporter, James Lyle.'

'Have you shown it to anyone else?'

'Only my immediate junior officers, both of whom are eminently trustworthy.'

'The editor, McGovern?'

'No, sir.'

'Good.' Strickland's inner turmoil was evident from his fast changing expressions, which ranged from near panic to harsh anger as he struggled to say the sort of thing he could retract. 'I want it.'

'Sorry, Sir Isaac. Even if I wanted to make a deal, which I don't, the list must be produced as an article in Lyle's possession during any trial for his murder.'

'Is that likely to be in the near future?'

Had Jarrett felt in any way kindly disposed to the man he might have put his mind at ease by telling that the person who killed Lyle was himself dead by his own hand. There would be no trial.

'Events change by the hour,' he said. 'As a matter of fact, you could clear up certain aspects of the crime by telling me exactly what happened in Darnwood Mansion.'

'To Lyle, you mean?' Strickland shrugged expansively. 'He was caught breaking and entering, I believe, and taken in front of Sir John Gordon of Darnwood. In my father's day he would have been given a thrashing and handed over to the law who, no doubt, would have given him another one. But these are enlightened times, Superintendent. Sir John accepted the fact that he was a newspaper man and not a burglar, and instructed his footmen to escort him from the premises, but not to harm him. He was last seen scurrying along the river path, no doubt greatly relieved to have been treated so mercifully.'

'Was he searched?'

'Do you think I would be negotiating for that confounded list if he had been? It never occurred to anyone that the little sneak had been spying on everyone who arrived by carriage.'

Having finally confirmed that Short and no one else had been responsible for the murder of James Lyle, Jarrett said, 'If there is nothing else, Sir Isaac . . . '

'Not so quick, Superintendent.' Since there was nothing else for it, Strickland steeled himself to bite the bullet and have done with the matter. 'I'm told you can't be bought.'

'I am willing to trade. Let me put it this way: I am more interested in solving a serious crime than in ruining a reputation. Unless it was in the interest of the community that would serve no useful purpose at all.'

'Good. I'm very glad to hear it. Now, if you tell me what you want, and I am in a position to grant it, I am sure we can strike a happy bargain.'

'I think you already know what I want — the identity and whereabouts of the Confederate.'

'Are you empowered to involve yourself in foreign wars, Superintendent?'

'As I understand it, they are at liberty to engage in warlike activities outwith British waters, but anything that happens on Sovereign territory is subject to the laws of the land. There are no exceptions. Foreigners cannot fight wars on our soil.'

Strickland nodded pensively.

'You are asking me to betray a trust,

Superintendent,' he said. 'What will that do for my standing?'

'No one need know, Sir Isaac.'

'I will have to take your word for that. There isn't much else I can do.' Strickland paused for a moment, then, 'I want two names removed from your list, Superintendent. Do you have it with you?'

'No, it's under lock and key in my office.'

'Then I must trust you to keep your word. I am assured that you are honourable and can ask for no more than that.'

'The names will be removed, Sir Isaac,' Jarrett offered, 'just as soon as your information has led to a conclusion of this matter.'

'Completely obliterated?'

'With Indian ink. Utterly impenetrable.'

'And how would you explain this in a court of law?'

'I would say it was in the interests of national security, Sir Isaac. No one would argue with that.'

'Very well.' Strickland mulled this over briefly before adding, 'The names concerned are my own, of course, and Mrs Parfrey, wife of Malcolm Parfrey of the Ship Bank.'

'And your connection with Mrs Parfrey . . . ?'

'She is my daughter.'

Superintendent Jarrett had been an officer

of the law for too long to be surprised by much. Strickland may have thought that he had been finally caught plumbing the black depths of depravity, when it fact it was scarcely worth a second thought. The whys and wherefores of it all were of no interest whatsoever to Henry Jarrett.

'Now the identity and hiding place of the killer, Sir Isaac, if you don't mind,' he said flatly. 'You must have been protecting him all along.'

'First, I want you to know that it wasn't through choice. I drew the short straw, Superintendent, it is that simple. A group of us have interests and properties in the Southern States which will be lost if the North wins. But until those Union men arrived with orders to kill the Confederate we were not actively involved in anything other than reading the papers and hoping for the best. As soon as Confederate spies in Washington found out about the assassination plot, however, all that changed. We had to protect our interests, and to do that we must ensure a supply of blockade runners to the South.'

'It isn't my place to take sides, or to judge, Sir Isaac. All I want is the whereabouts of the one they call the Ghost.'

Strickland raised his eyebrows in surprise.

'Now, that is very interesting,' he said. 'Very few people know the Pinkerton codename. You seem to be party to more information than was originally thought. Perhaps it is time to look out for myself.'

'Not a moment too soon, Sir Isaac.'

'In that case the man you are looking for is Lieutenant Amos Mallory. For the last month he has been living in a deserted church house in the Kelvin valley. I will even draw a map showing you exactly how to find it.'

Superintendent Jarrett waited until the Kinross wagon was quite some way down the tree-lined driveway before taking the neatly sketched map from his waistcoat pocket and considering how best to approach the place. Mallory was clearly not the sort of man who would be taken easily or without a fight, so perhaps it was just as well that Charlie Grant and Tommy Quinn had gone off for a bit of rest. Later, when dusk settled on the vale, they would need their wits about them.

In the meantime, partly because he had a few hours to kill and partly because Rattray may have been planning to suspend or dismiss him for investigating the shipyard after being told not to, Henry Jarrett decided to attend to the Edgar Trimmer affair.

* * *

On this particular occasion, it fell to Henry Jarrett to let Mrs Maitland know that a wagon would be calling for him at eight o'clock. Between the evening meal and that hour the Trimmer business would have to be resolved. He did not mention the forthcoming raid or the possibility of an armed siege.

Edgar Trimmer had been lulled into a false sense of security at dinner by Jarrett's smiling nod and the gracious attentions of Elsie Maitland. So the last thing he expected as he sat on the edge of the bed and tugged open his boot-laces was a thrown-back door and the superintendent's silhouette in the gaslit doorway. He could not see Mrs Maitland to the right in the corridor, where she had been instructed to keep Sweetman and Croall away from things that did not concern them. They would soon know as much as they needed to, but that would be after everything had been taken care of and the dust had settled.

'I wouldn't do that if I were you, Trimmer,' Jarrett said coldly. 'You're going to need your boots.'

The bookseller unthinkingly caught the bundled bedsheet, then stared at it without the least comprehension. He had absolutely no idea what was happening, or what was about to happen.

'I don't . . . '

'Open it out on the floor. Do it now.'

There was no need for a repeat order. Trimmer dropped to his knees and made as good a job of spreading out the sheet as might be expected, and that was far from perfect.

'May I ask — ?' he began.

'No you may not. You will do as you are told or face the consequences.' Jarrett pointed at the large wardrobe. 'Bring down those boxes and place them on the bed.'

Trimmer got quickly to his feet and fetched down the large mahogany case, then two smaller ones and a long, leather-strapped tripod. These he set out on the bed before turning to Henry Jarrett and spreading his arms in a gesture of submission.

'It's my equipment,' he said needlessly. 'What do you want me to do?'

'Open them.'

The largest of the boxes was lined with red velvet and contained an expensive half-plate camera of polished wood and gleaming brass. The others, also lined in red, held assorted lenses. The three section tripod was unboxed.

'These are extremely expensive items,' Trimmer offered. 'If you are going to handle them, please do so with care.'

'No harm will come to your apparatus, Trimmer. Now, where are the plates?'

Trimmer stared at him for a moment, then said, 'I don't have any prepared plates at the moment.'

'Bring out the material.'

There was a brief moment of hesitation on Trimmer's part, then he drew open one of the wardrobe doors and pulled out another wooden box, this one rougher in construction and packed with straw.

'It's collodion,' he said respectfully. 'Do you know what that is?'

'Gun cotton.'

'Yes, dissolved in ethyl alcohol and ethyl ether.'

'And highly explosive if exposed to a naked flame.'

Trimmer blinked, but at least some vague explanation for this intrusion was rattling around in his mind.

'Is that what this is all about?' he whispered hoarsely. 'My God, there are countless photographers in this and every city. Why pick on me?'

The idea that Trimmer was storing material that could conceivably threaten life and limb was less than pleasing to Jarrett. But that was not the issue, merely one more unpleasant factor in Trimmer's overall wickedness.

'I am going to tell you one more time,' the Superintendent said. 'Bring out the plates.'

Slowly, but surely, the real truth was beginning to dawn. This had nothing to do with collodion and gas lights. The initial shock Trimmer had experienced when Jarrett made his dramatic entrance had completely unnerved and confused him, but now it was all crystal clear: it was connected with the unjustifiable invasion of his bookshop and the entirely unwarranted removal of his gentleman's art. But, whatever the reason for his present nightmare, there was no way out. He was beginning to feel nauseous and very frightened.

Since further argument would serve no purpose and would probably go unheard, he drew open the other wardrobe door and produced a strawboard box that proved to be heavier than its size suggested because it contained only glass plates.

'Empty them onto the sheet,' Jarrett ordered. 'Tie the corners.'

Trimmer tipped the box, paused for a few moments while he sought some way out of the mess, then slowly permitted the half-plate negatives to spill out until the strawboard box was empty and his precious originals lay in a heap. Then, as instructed, he collected the corners of the worn and discarded cotton sheet and made a pauper's bundle.

'That's it,' he said huffily. 'It's all there is.'

'Then pick it up and follow me.'

Sweetman and Croall probably had some idea of what was going on but, as they watched the miserable Trimmer lugging his rattling sack along the upper corridor, with Superintendent Jarrett leading the way like an executioner on his way to the thirteen steps, the exact nature of Edgar Trimmer's crime still eluded them.

By the time they reached the foot of the stairs, had passed through the narrow passage to the kitchen, then progressed beyond that to the courtyard at the rear of the house, Trimmer was close to fainting. But his labours were not finished yet.

Jarrett indicated a sledgehammer leaning against the outhouse wall.

'Get to it,' he said. 'I don't want to see a bit larger than a thumbnail when you're finished.'

It took about fifteen minutes of rare and unaccustomed effort on Trimmer's part before Henry Jarrett was satisfied that nothing remained that could be of the slightest use to a peddler of such trash. The bundle was then unceremoniously dumped on the midden and the heavy hammer returned to its rightful place in the tool store.

'Are we finished?' Trimmer asked, the first signs of his old arrogance creeping back into his tone. It had occurred to him that he had just been forced to destroy the evidence, so a prosecution was obviously not planned. 'If so, I would like to return to my room now.'

'Of course you may,' Jarrett replied. 'We both will.'

Accompanied by Superintendent Jarrett, a mildly confused Edgar Trimmer retraced his steps until he was again standing by the bed and watching his tormentor examining a 'Gem' portrait lens.

'That cost me a considerable amount of money,' Trimmer pointed out. 'Please don't damage it.'

'I have no intention of doing so.' Jarrett placed the lens carefully into its individual box and closed the lid on it. 'You know, Trimmer, this equipment is better than the few bits and pieces we have to hand.'

The bookseller stared at Jarrett, then at his prized possessions.

'I hope you are not suggesting . . . '

'I was merely making an observation.' Jarrett closed in on him and peered into those little piggy eyes. 'Such apparatus would be better put to use in the fight against crime, rather than the production of depraved filth. Wouldn't it be better to do good for once, instead of being dragged into court on a vile charge?'

Trimmer was shaking with anger now.

'You have nothing on me, nothing you could use to force me to give up my equipment. The negatives are gone and you have no proof at all.'

'I wasn't referring to your disgusting photographs, Trimmer. I was talking about your treatment of Lizzie Gill.'

'You couldn't prove that. It would be her word against mine.'

'Not exactly. If Detective Constable Williamson, Sergeant Quinn and I were to give evidence on her behalf you would almost certainly be sent to Duke Street prison. It is quite clear from the photographs that she was not a willing subject.' Jarrett reached into his coat pocket and produced the six half-plate prints of Miss Elizabeth Gill. He fanned them like playing cards. 'They even have your handwriting on the back.'

Trimmer was speechless and trapped. Had there been the slightest chink of light he would have made for it, but there was nothing, no way out.

'This is stealing,' he said feebly.

'Not at all. I merely asked you to consider donating the equipment to the photographic unit of the Detective Department. We have great difficulty getting funding for anything and this would be very much appreciated.'

'Very well.' Trimmer clearly accepted the fact that he had no choice. 'On the understanding that the other matter will go no further.'

'Naturally. The very last thing I would wish to do is put the young lady through such an ordeal, but I would do if you were less than co-operative.' Jarrett allowed this to sink in. 'Now, if this were my house I would throw you out, but sadly it isn't. However, I believe Mrs Maitland has a few words to say to you.'

'There won't be any need for that.' Trimmer dropped quickly to his knees and fetched a large valise from beneath the bed. This he began to fill with shirts, spare johns and various items from his small chest of drawers. 'You don't think I could stay here now, do you? How could I sit in the dining-room with those bastards staring at me all the time? Imagine having to endure Croall's disapproving glare. And as for that fat rodent, Sweetman, well I would never hear the last of it. Just how many vulgar jokes do you think he could wring out of it?'

'Quite a number I should imagine, but I doubt if even the most depraved remarks could shock you.'

Trimmer paused briefly in the open doorway.

'You have ruined me, Jarrett,' he snapped,

'but no doubt that pleases you.'

'Nothing about this affair pleases me. Certainly not the ruination of Lizzie Gill.'

It was something between a sharp laugh and a snort.

'You can't be that naïve. Truth is, you would have to go back a long time to pinpoint that historic moment.'

Then Trimmer was gone, sweeping past Elsie Maitland, whose prepared speech must forever remain unsaid, and on down the stairs to the hall. The slamming of the glass-panelled front door was followed by a prolonged silence before Banker Croall said, 'Well, there's a fine kettle of fish, don't you know.'

* * *

Jarrett, Grant, Quinn and Constable MacLean left the Kinross wagon and proceeded on foot. Although it was not yet 8.30 p.m., the cloud-obscured moon and absence of stars meant that visibility was limited to no more than three or four yards. But it hadn't always been like this. Only a generation or so ago this was a weavers' village, its paths and lanes clearly illuminated by oil lamps until well into the night. But progress had killed all that.

The only way they could approach the old

church house unseen was by ascending a sparsely wooded slope to the rear of the overgrown burial ground. It was larger and a whole lot muddier, but it finally took them to a part of the crumbling perimeter wall that was out of sight of the two-storey building beside the disused church. There they paused to consider exactly what they were going to do and how to do it.

'Inspector,' Jarrett whispered hoarsely, 'you and Sergeant Quinn skirt round to the rear of the house, just in case he tries to make a run for it. But for God's sake don't block his path. He may have the makila in his hand.'

Jarrett waited until his officers had disappeared into the murk, then counted to ten as he took the Adams revolver from his pocket. He felt a shudder pass through him as he remembered how the three Union men had been struck down, swiftly and without warning. What had been going through Mallory's mind then? He couldn't have known if they were armed, so did he think he was bullet-proof, or invisible? Suddenly Jarrett realized that he was thinking about the agent as though the man was some kind of insane killer, when in fact he was nothing of the sort. He was merely highly trained, dedicated and very dangerous.

It was ten long paces to the wall of the

ancient church. Closely followed by young MacLean, Henry Jarrett took it in the same number of paces, pressed himself against the cold stone for a few moments, then crept around the end of the building and stopped only when he had reached the paved area between the church and the house. After pausing briefly, they crossed the exposed area and again braced themselves beside the first window of the house, the gun still in Jarrett's hand and ready for the first sign of ambush.

The room within was in virtual darkness, but as Jarrett gained his night eyes he could just make out that it was plainly furnished and seemingly devoid of life. Signalling to MacLean, he moved past the window and the plain front door to the second window, yet there was still no sign of occupancy. Only when he was as close as possible to being satisfied that Mallory was not lying in wait for him did he gently, but firmly, press the butt of the Adams against the sun-dried putty all round the small pane of glass immediately above the window catch. Little by little, the aged material crumbled and fell away, until the glass was barely held in place by four tiny and badly rusted nails. It was only necessary to bend the top two out of shape for the pane to lean forward and be easily removed. The catch was equally inefficient and within a minute or so he was able to raise the sash window far enough to allow him to snake in head first, but if anyone was inclined to decapitate a detective superintendent they would never have a better opportunity. A lesser man might have ordered the young constable to lead the way, but that sort of thing was not in Henry Jarrett's book. It was no way to gain respect.

The house did not really merit much in the way of security. It was not only simple, but sparse, yet such furniture as there was could not have survived from the days when the village was alive. It had either been carted here recently for Amos Mallory's benefit, or it had other, prior uses. Jarrett touched the black grate and found it just warm and no more. He crossed to the door and opened it to reveal a narrow hallway and the doors to the three other rooms, two which he had already determined were empty by the simple expedient of peering through the windows. But just in case he investigated each. All of them, including the third one which turned out to be little more than a box room, were devoid of life.

A wealthier church house might have had a stained-glass window on the half-landing, or at least plain frosted, but here it was just a bare wall without so much as a tiny skylight.

The result was a pitch-black upper hall. Constable MacLean flicked open the curved door of his bull's-eye lamp, struck a lucifer on the wall and applied the flame to the heavy wick. Almost immediately, the inch-thick lens sent out an expanding beam of yellow light that illuminated every corner and crevice.

Suddenly, there was a crash of heavy timber and almost immediately a yell. Somewhere down below Sergeant Quinn was shouting for assistance. Jarrett turned on a tread and brushed past young MacLean, who quickly followed him as he retraced his steps, the harsh light of the lamp ensuring that every step was true and that there was no fear of stumbling.

Charlie Grant was on his knees, his forehead touching the cold stone of the kitchen floor. Tommy Quinn, who was kneeling and had one hand on the Inspector's back, looked up at Jarrett.

'He came out of nowhere,' he said. 'He must have been in the pantry. As soon as Inspector Grant shouldered the door in he came out on the charge.'

Jarrett felt immediately nauseous.

'Has Charlie been stabbed?' he asked, dreading the reply.

'No, he hit him on the side of the head, probably with that makila thing.

'Thank God for that.' But as soon as Jarrett said it came the realization that a medlar-wood cosh, even without the drawn blade, was hard enough to do a great deal of damage, and could prove fatal.

'I'm fine.' Charlie Grant sat back on his heels and braced himself on the roughcast wall. 'You had better get after him, sir. He has a good start on you now.'

'Are you sure you're all right?'

'Couldn't be better.' Grant smiled thinly at the blood smears on his fingers. It was coming from the thick hair at his right temple and trickling into his sideburn. 'Get on, now. I'll hobble along as best I can.'

Henry Jarrett patted the inspector on the shoulder and immediately launched himself out through the ragged doorway, closely followed by Constable MacLean. After a few moments, when it became apparent that Grant did not want nursemaiding, Tommy Quinn joined the chase. Lacking the youthful vigour of either MacLean or Quinn, Jarrett soon found both level with him and suspected that he might even be holding them back.

'Go on, lads,' he shouted, 'catch him. But be careful for God's sake.'

Then he was alone, but trying his best to keep sight of MacLean's lamp. That way there would be less chance of running into a tree or derelict cottage in the murk and laying himself out, possibly briefly, perhaps forever.

Although it had taken quite some time to reach the cottage in the first place, the descent was extremely rapid. It was only a matter of minutes before the ill-kempt road was again reached and MacLean and Quinn were running no more. The former was keeping the yellow beam on the figure lying on the rutted hardpack, while the latter knelt beside the fallen man.

'It's Constable Watson, sir,' Quinn informed the superintendent. 'He is still breathing. Didn't have a chance if you ask me.'

Jarrett raised his hand in a request for silence. The wagon was moving quickly and beginning to fade into the distance. Mallory, it seemed, was as adept with the ribbons as he was with a club and a dagger.

There seemed little point to pursuing a wagon and pair, so Jarrett waited until Charlie Grant eventually arrived and Constable Watson regained consciousness before all five set off in various states of awareness in the direction of the main Dalmarnock Road. Once there they would at least have their bearings.

They found the wagon some forty minutes later. It was just sitting there, waiting for them, with the horses tethered to a low branch and no sign at all of Amos Mallory.

* * *

At eight o'clock the following morning, Henry Jarrett hung his coat on the horn rack as per usual and took his rightful place behind the desk. But he was more than conscious of the possibility of Rattray demanding his brass badge. Indeed, he earnestly anticipated it. His investigation of the Tod and MacGregor shipyard after being ordered to drop the case was in itself sufficient reason for the chief constable to suspend or remove him. Mishandling a raid and inadvertently causing injury to two police officers made it virtually certain. At any moment a young constable who probably felt that he was doomed to carry folds of paper up and down the stairs for the rest of his life, would appear at the doorway with a handwritten order for Jarrett to present himself in the CC's office.

Just then the constable did arrive, but not with instructions from above.

'This arrived a few minutes ago,' he said apologetically. 'It is addressed to you. It was posted at five this morning.'

Jarrett lifted his paper knife and cut the

thin twine that secured the small box. On lifting the lid he first encountered wood wool packing, then snuggling securely within was a black, medlar-wood makila. The note was brief and to the point. 'To Superintendent Jarrett for his collection if he has one, or as a first exhibit if he has not. Amos Mallory CSN.'

He was still toying with the note when Charlie Grant and Tommy Quinn arrived. Sergeant Quinn, as always, was bright and cheery and almost ready for another day. Only the possibility of Jarrett's departure dampened his mood. Inspector Grant's head was giving him gyp and he wasn't ready for anything. He read the offered note, then passed it on to Quinn.

'Heard from the gods, sir?' Grant asked.

'I'm expecting to do so at any second,' Jarrett admitted. Then he addressed Quinn. 'While we're waiting, Sergeant, find out if there have been any sailings from Glasgow since five this morning.'

Tommy Quinn was absent for less than ten minutes.

'Good guess, sir,' he announced. 'Steamship *Caroline*.'

'Bound for?'

'New York.'

Charlie Grant looked somewhat quizzical.

'That's enemy territory for him, Superintendent.'

'So? A spy can't achieve very much at home, can he?'

'Might be a bluff. He could have sent you the weapon and note, then gone into hiding knowing that we would jump to the obvious conclusion.'

'No, Inspector, he's gone. If I were a gambling man I would bet you a sovereign that the three ships have been paid for and will in due time be delivered to the Azores, and there is nothing in the world anyone can do about that. I think we can safely assume that Mallory is finished here.'

It was then that the summons came from on high, but it was not in the form of a note on this occasion. The nervous young constable chapped the door, entered when instructed, and said, 'The Chief Constable would like to see you, Superintendent. He said now, if you please.'

Jarrett rose from his seat and tugged his waistcoat straight.

'Anything to get on with, gentlemen?' he enquired.

Grant and Quinn exchanged glances.

'Not a lot,' Charlie Grant replied. 'A couple of floaters taken from the Clyde, the odd possible murder or two and a few dozen assaults.'

'Plus a wages robbery and a pickpocket gang working the department stores,' Tommy Quinn added.

'A quiet day, in fact,' Jarrett said warmly, as he left the office. 'Don't let all this leisure go to your heads, lads. Business will soon pick up again.'

Under normal circumstances Chief Constable Rattray would have been found posing at the window, where onlookers on the office building opposite could see him and assume that he was keeping an eye on his city. On this occasion even that pretence went by the board. He was too busy boxing his books and various knick-knacks, none of which had anything whatsoever to do with police work. But then neither had he.

'You've done for me, Jarrett,' he said gruffly but not too loud. 'The Lord Advocate wants my resignation by five o'clock this evening; you are finished as from now.'

'Now . . . ?'

'Effective immediately.' The CC glared hard at him. 'I told you to quit, but you just couldn't back off, could you? Now you have shown yourself to be an enemy of the merchants, and by association so have I. To their way of thinking I must have instructed you to make a pest of yourself at the shipyard and elsewhere.'

'Perhaps if you called upon your friends, sir.'

'I don't have any friends. Not now. I'll be a pariah wherever I go. I planned to build a villa in Dunoon or Rothesay, but now I'll be lucky if they let me sell tickets on the pier.'

'At the risk of repeating myself,' Jarrett said softly, while digging in his inside pocket for what was fast becoming a well-worn sheet of lined paper, 'I think you should call on your friends.'

Rattray took the sheet and frowned at it.

'This is?'

'The now infamous Lyle list, Chief Constable.' Jarrett nodded happily. 'You must have heard rumours of its existence. A great number of people have been quaking in their boots since Jimmy Lyle wrote this. It is a list of those who attended the frivolities, for the want of a better word, at Darnwood Mansion.'

'Is it, indeed?' Rattray took the paper to the window and chuckled to himself. 'My God, there are names here to be reckoned with. Who would have thought it?'

'At least two judges, sir, and half of the Chamber of Commerce.'

Rattray stared at Jarrett for quite some

time, then said, 'You thought you would find my name on this, didn't you, Jarrett?'

'Perish the thought, sir.'

'Don't give me that. You'd have had me by the bloody olives.' Rattray shuddered as someone walked over his grave. 'Just imagine what life would be like if Mrs Rattray found out I had been at something like this.'

'That's precisely the position these poor gentlemen find themselves in, sir.'

'Yes they do, don't they?' Rattray laughed and tapped the paper. 'Two obliterations, Jarrett. What is this?'

'Just an understanding. Assistance rendered, sir.'

'I see.' Chief Constable Rattray returned to his desk and pushed the half-filled box aside. Wouldn't be needing that any more. 'We have never really seen eye-to-eye, Jarrett, but I have to admit you're a cunning bugger. Deep down I just knew you wouldn't sink this day.'

'Thank you, sir. So did I.'

'Much as it grieves me to say this, Jarrett, but I can't think of anyone I'd rather have as chief of detectives.'

'Again, thank you, sir. And if you don't mind me saying so you are exactly what I want in a chief constable,'

'Really?' Rattray was momentarily pleased, then confusion set in. 'Am I?'

We do hope that you have enjoyed reading this large print book.

Did you know that all of our titles are available for purchase?

We publish a wide range of high quality large print books including:
Romances, Mysteries, Classics
General Fiction
Non Fiction and Westerns

Special interest titles available in large print are:
The Little Oxford Dictionary
Music Book
Song Book
Hymn Book
Service Book

Also available from us courtesy of Oxford University Press:
Young Readers' Dictionary
(large print edition)
Young Readers' Thesaurus
(large print edition)

For further information or a free brochure, please contact us at:
Ulverscroft Large Print Books Ltd.,
The Green, Bradgate Road, Anstey,
Leicester, LE7 7FU, England.
Tel: (00 44) **0116 236 4325**
Fax: (00 44) **0116 234 0205**